P.C. Murdoch says:

> Now then you young uns –
> We're not wanting any accidents!

This book of Oor Wullie's is packed with things to do.

Some of them might seem a bit old-fashioned, and some of them could be a bit dangerous if you don't take care.

If you're making something, get permission to use the tools, learn how to use them safely and get help with difficult bits.

Never play with matches.

Always tell your Ma or Pa or a grown-up what you're up to.

When you're out and about follow

The Scottish Outdoor Access Code:

- Take responsibility for your own actions
- Respect people's privacy and peace of mind
- Help farmers, landowners and others to work safely and effectively
- Care for the environment
- Keep your dog under proper control
- Take extra care if you are organising a group, an event or running a business

OOR WULLIE'S

DUNGAREES

BOOK

for Boys

WAVERLEY BOOKS

Oor Wullie's Dungarees Book For Boys is published 2010
by Waverley Books Ltd, 144 Port Dundas Road, Glasgow, Scotland, G4 OHZ.

Produced by Waverley Books Ltd, Text © 2010 Waverley Books and
D.C. Thomson & Co. Ltd.
The Oor Wullie logo, characters and cartoon strips appear courtesy of, and are
®© DC Thomson & Co. Ltd. 2010

Text is by Waverley Books, Christopher Riches, and Martin Haston, advised by David
Donaldson and Morris Heggie, the Oor Wullie scriptwriters.

Design, layout and additional artwork by Hugo Breingan.

The publishers wish to thank Jim Cooper for use of items from his collection of
memorabilia.

Selected images used are registered trademarks ® and are copyright ©:
p 73, ® Airfix (©Hornby Hobbies Ltd), p 90, ® Heinz (© H J Heinz Co Ltd); p 97, ® KitKat
(Rowntrees, ©Nestlé UK Ltd); p 98, ® Wagon Wheels (©Burton's Foods Ltd); p 98, ® Fry's
(© Kraft Foods UK Ltd); p 98, ® Bazooka (© Topps Europe Ltd); p 98, ® Maltesers (© Mars
Ltd); p 140, ® Scott's Porage Oats (© Quaker Oats Ltd); p 186, ® Aero (Rowntrees, © Nestlé UK
Ltd); p 186, ® Nestlé's (© Nestlé UK Ltd); p 187, ® Wall's (© Unilever UK); p 187, ® Milky Way
(© Mars Ltd); p, 187, ® Barratt's (© Kraft Foods UK Ltd).
p 138/9 Highland Games images © 2010 Famedram Publishers Ltd.
Additional items used are from The Hotspur ®©, The Topper ®© The Wizard ®©
The Beezer ®© and The Sparky © DC Thomson & Co Ltd.
The Ten Shilling Note is reproduced by permission of Bank of England.
Additional graphics by arrangement with Shutterstock.

We are very grateful to the many organisations and individuals for permission to reproduce
photographs and illustrations in this book. We have made every effort to contact the
copyright holders of reproduced material.
For any queries or suggestions, please contact us.

ISBN: 978 1 84934 033 5

Printed and bound in the EU.

10 - 9 - 8 - 7 - 6 - 5 - 4 - 3 - 2 - 1

WULLIE'S WISDOMS

Who says ye
cannae judge a
book by its cover?

Welcome tae ma book

Jings, I never expected tae write that. Books, I thocht, are only written by fowk like Specky Spence. Then Ma wis tellin' me that there wis so much in ma heid that it were near full tae burstin'. So I got tae thinkin' that I'd better get it a' oot o' ma heid and write it doon in this book.

Whit a job! It wis only when Pa said that I could sell the book that I saw the point o' a' the work.

So here's ma book wi' lots o' things tae do, tae mak' an' tae enjoy.

I'll even let ye into ma secrets on how tae raise funds — but only if ye buy this book, ye ken!

(signed)
Wullie

Publisher

Bucket Books

3

THINGS YE NEED TAE
MAK' A BOOK

SCRAPBOOK WI'
COLOURED PAGES
PEN, CRAYONS,
SCISSORS
GLUE, STAPLER, AULD
MAGAZINES
LOTS O' IDEAS,
PHOTOGRAPHS
DRAWINGS

Me ~~writtin'~~ writin' carefully in ma book

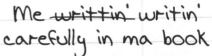

ALFA ROMEO

AUSTIN HEALEY 3000

E-TYPE JAGUAR

CHEVROLET CORVETTE

WHA'S IN MA BOOK

THE BEGINNIN'

THE END

Jist tae help a'body who dinnae ken the important fowk in ma life, here are a few wee mug shots tae help ye identify them.

WULLIE'S WISDOMS

Better a guid name than a pretty face.

Me, o' course

Primrose
Fermer Tam
Auld McTavish
Uncle Joe
Aunty Joan
Jeemy

Oh, an' Joey, ma wee Goldfish.

Ma

Pa

Soapy Soutar

Wee Eck

Fat Bob

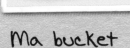

Ma bucket

P.C. Murdoch

Harry – ma dug

Granpaw Broon

6

PART 1 - Aboot me

I LIKE
MA CARTIE
OOTDOORS
MA CATTIE
JEEMY

I DINNA LIKE
SCHOOL
FACE WASHIN'
P.C. MURDOCH
    (only jokin')

me

Name. **Wullie**
Address. Auchenshoogle
.... Scotland
.... United Kingdom
.... The World
.... The Universe
.... The Galaxy
Number........ 1........ Signed **Wullie**

GLEN
15 FEB 1962
LIBRARY

No. 040 029 191   Expires   18 JAN 2001

William

IS ENTITLED TO BORROW BOOKS FROM
Auchenshoogle Public Library
2 High Street
AND IS RESPONSIBLE FOR ALL BOOKS TAKEN ON THIS CARD

DUE	RETURNED	DUE	RETURNED
14 FEB 1995	14 FEB 1995		
05 JUNE 1998		08 MAR 99	
Fined 60p:		Paid in full	
Overdue payment 1d			
Paid			

AUCHENSHOOGLE POLICE STATION
DATE *Thursday 15th*
POLICE CONSTABLE ...*Murdoch*.......

As I went about my patrol this morning, my helmet was knocked off, causing me great loss of dignity. The chief suspect is William (otherwise known as Oor Wullie).

Distinguishing features:

Blonde, spikey hair.
Wears dungarees all the time.
Has the noisiest tacketty boots in town.
Frequently seen sitting on his tin bucket.

Photos I didna use for ma ID card

Had tae keep this hidden fae Ma 'til she wis in a guid mood. →

Swimmer No. **192815**

Name ...... *William*

HAS RESERVED ADMISSION TO

Auchenshoogle Public Swimming Baths

From | To
08 MAR 95 | **MAR 13 1995**

This card is non-transferable. Card has no cash value. May not be re-sold, lent or hired. Non adherence of Terms & Conditions will result in card being made void.

Ma pass tae watery fun.

Auchenshoogle School

School Report

Student Name ...... *William* ...... Date *1 June*

Subject:

ENGLISH:	Comment
Mark **D**	*William is a dreadful speller. His English is attrocious.*

HISTORY	Comment
Mark **D-**	*He is at the foot of the class in History.*

MATHS:	Comment
Mark **D-**	*Reasonable at counting the cost of sweets!*

GEOGRAPHY:	Comment
Mark **D-**	*Geographical knowledge is confined to the location of football fields and Kelly Burn*

PHYSICAL EDUCATION:	Comment
Mark **A+**	*William is the best footballer we have. A first rate gymnast.*

Teacher's Signature ...... *Miss Matheson* ...... Date *1 June*

Further comments:

William seems to be an expert angler. (worm with bent pin method)

He knows more about practical jokes than the whole school put together!

Ma dungarees

Dungarees are the best clothes a laddie can hae. Here are jist a few reasons why.

A place tae keep Jeemy.

A place tae carry ma comics when I want a game o' headers.

A chance tae stand like the foreman an' his mate when they're diggin' the road.

A place tae carry apples awa' fae Grouser Green's orchard.

Things I can carry in ma dungarees:

"Could ye dae some invisible mending on ma dungarees?"

"Let's see your money first", said the tailor.

"There ye are."

"B-But there's nothing there!"

"Aye - it's invisible money!"

CATTIE
BOOLS
PENS
SWEETS
LUNCH
RULER

Ma tried tae get me tae wear jeans or shorts or a kilt! Nae sense in any o' them. There's nae place tae put anything.

Ma boots

Ma says I would sleep in ma tacketty boots if I could. Ma feet are jist made for them! Ye can dae a' sorts o' things wi' a good pair o' boots.

Ye can kick a fitba'

an' pull a cartie

an' dae Hieland dancin'

an' run

an' splash in puddles

an' hae a rest
(tho' Ma wasnae pleased).

WULLIE! GET OFF O' THERE WI' YER MUDDY BOOTS.

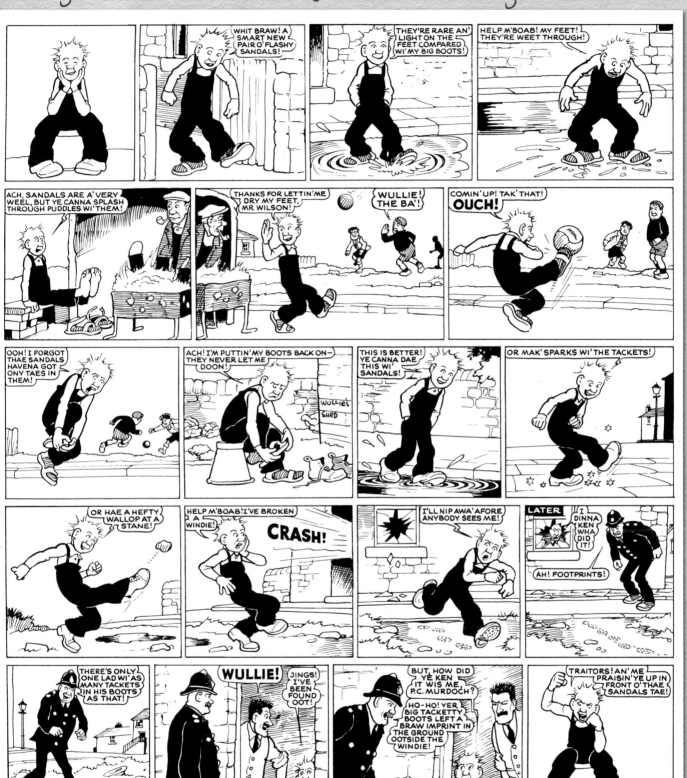

Ma bucket

Ye cannae separate me fae ma bucket. It's the maist useful thing in the world. I'll give ye 101 different uses throughout the book (though as numbers isnae ma strong point, I may lose count...). The maist important thing aboot buckets is that ye must use a metal bucket - no' ae o' thon plastic things.

No.14

YE CAN MAK BIGGER
SAND CASTLES THAN
FAT BOAB'S WEE PAIL!

Quality heavy-duty
metal bucket. The
← business!

BEWARE o' "pail"
imitations.

Ye'll find these
cards a' through
this book.

Ma bucket.   Fat Bob's
                  bucket.

Biggest
sandcastles on
the beach.

Ancestral buckets

Wee Jock McWullie wis the best poacher in the land.

Ae day, Jock wis seen by the gamie an' had tae run for his life.

He wis crawlin' under a fence when his breeks got caught, so he had tae leave them.

He hid in thon cave up on Stoorie Hill an' sat on an auld bucket thinkin' how tae get hame.

Suddenly he had an idea. He knocked the bottom oot o' the bucket an' next minute oot came Jock wearin' the bucket!

Jock's bucket saved the day. He got back hame safe an' sound.

And that's why ye'll find a bucket in every McWullie backyard tae this day.

Fat Bob got a free plastic bucket fae the grocers.

> HUH! IT'S JUST A PLASTIC BUCKET — NO' A REAL TIN ANE LIKE MINE!

> IT HAUDS WATER — AN' THAT'S MAIR THAN YOUR AULD LEAKY BUCKET CAN DAE!

Buckets today

There's still nothin' tae beat the tin bucket. These plastic things cannae dae the jobs a tin bucket can. Jist look at ma list o' things ye canna use a plastic bucket for.

We had a competishun tae see wha's bucket wis best.

Test. Run around the block wi' a bucket full o' water an' the person wi' the maist water left in the bucket wins.

THINKING

PLASTIC BUCKETS ARE NAE USE FOR:

CARRYIN' HOT CINDERS — WILL MELT

FOR KEEPIN' YE WARM WHEN FILLED WI' HOT COALS OR HOT WATER — DISNAE GIE OOT HEAT

FOR SITTIN' ON — NAE STRANG ENUFF FOR FAT BOB

COOKIN' IN WHEN CAMPIN' — WILL MELT

USIN' AS A DRUM — DISNA MAK' A GUID SOUND

USIN' AS A MIRROR — CANNAE POLISH PLASTIC TAE SEE YOUR FACE

> THE RACE OVER.

> HERE! YOUR WATER'S FROZEN! THAT'S NO' FAIR! YOU MUST HAVE HAD IT IN THE BUTCHER'S FRIDGE.

> WELL, IT'S STILL WATER, ISN'T IT?

ICE

½ EMPTY

101 THINGS TAE DAE WI' A BUCKET

No. 100 ANITHER BUCKET TAE KEEP YER GUID ANE CLEAN.

Ma bucket's full o' holes. Whit shall I dae? The next day we ran roond the block an' I won. Ma bucket wis full o' ice!

Fat Bob lost an' I won his bucket — an' it does hae a use, as a cover for ma tin bucket!

Ma shed

I wis banned fae playin' quietly in the hoose which I thocht wis awfy unfair. So a'thing that could possibly cause damage or mak' the least bit o' noise wis moved tae the shed.
That's how it became Wullie's Shed.
I wis a bit pit oot at first, but I came roond tae thinkin' it wis better tae hae ma ain place richt in ma ain back yard – a hame fae hame.
Somewhere jist tae get awa' an' relax, or get on wi' stuff in peace wi'oot bein' tellt tae stop it or tidy up.

OCH! THE MICE MUST HAVE BEEN AT IT! THEY'VE CHEWED UP A' THE TAIL!

I hae tae keep it clean an' tidy mind, an' clean up every week an' my precious stuff needs tae be in wooden boxes an' wrapped up well, cos there's field mice aboot. There's nothin' they like better than a wee feed on ma toys!

Uses for ma shed

The maist important thing aboot the shed is it's whaur we hae oor gang meetin's.

The next maist important thing is that it is whaur I dae a' ma inventin' an' buildin'.

Piece an' quiet!

*PASSWORD FOR GANG MEMBERS TAE GET INTAE WULLIE'S SHED IS: JEEMY

It's a great place tae test new stuff.

But it's a multi funkshanal space. I dae haircuts in it. For half the price that the barber does. Guid business!

The shed's whaur Jeemy lives at nicht. Ma will no' hae a moose in the hoose.

I hae exhibishuns an' charge fowk tae get in.

It's a gallery as weel!

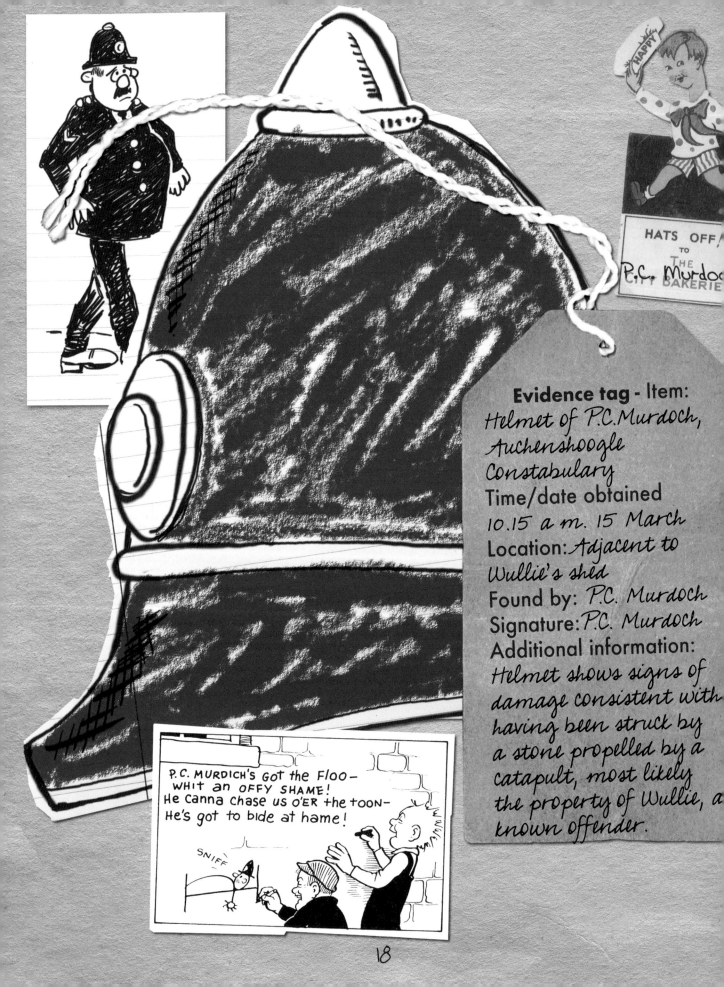

How many ways can ye knock
P.C. Murdoch's helmet aff?

AUCHENSHOOGLE POLICE STATION

DATE .. 21st December

POLICE CONSTABLE .. Murdoch

*As I went around on my beat
today, my helmet was knocked off
three times. For each incident I
suspect the culprits are those young
scamps Wullie and Fat Bob.
The first incident was effected by
means of a catapult and a stone.
The second incident was by a bow
and arrow (fitted with a sucker)
and the third incident was at
the petrol station, when an air
hose used to pump up tyres was
employed to blow my helmet off.*

WAYS TAE KNOCK
P.C. MURDOCH'S
HELMET AFF:
CATTIE ✓
APPLE
MAGNET ✗
(DISNAE WORK)
BOW AN' ARROW ✓
PEA SHOOTER ✓
AIR HOSE ✓

Tae practise ye
can use tin cans
on a wall or ye
could mak' a model
heid in Plasticine. →

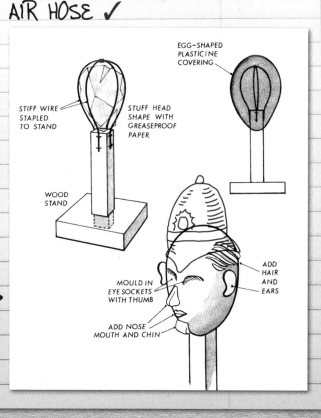

Now I've a'ready stuck in a page fae P.C. Murdoch's Note Book. How did I get that? Weel . . . I found a book that had been drapped in the road. It wis P.C. Murdoch's Note Book!

I took a quick keek, an' found ma name in it! Whit should I dae?

Should I
- bury it?
- burn it?
- toss it in a dustbin?
- drop it in a river?
- tear the pages oot aboot me?

Then I kent whit tae dae.

AUCHENSHOOGLE CONSTABULARY

P.C. Murdoch

AUCHENSHOOGLE POLICE STATION
DATE .... 4th November ....
POLICE CONSTABLE ..... Murdoch ....

Mister Green complains that Wullie has been setting up cheek to him again.

But he's no' a bad lad reely, he wis only stickin' up for hissel an' rite after it he wis helpin' Mrs Mutch ower the road then he carried Mrs Munro's parcels an' gave his last peppery tae a starvin' dog. Whit mair could ye ask?

An' he gave me the ither pages that had ma name on too!

20

101 THINGS TAE DAE WI' A BUCKET

No. 11 CARRYING COAL THAT'S FALLEN OFF THE BACK OF A LORRY.

AUCHENSHOOGLE POLICE STATION
DATE Tuesday 23rd
POLICE CONSTABLE Murdoch

Saturday – The Chief Inspector of Police is coming to inspect this afternoon. He wants to see how the youth policy is getting on. Need to have stern words with Wullie and the rest to ensure there are no breaches of the peace. These lads need to know who is in charge around here, and I'm not to be made a fool of.

AUCHENSHOOGLE POLICE STATION
DATE Wednesday 25th
POLICE CONSTABLE Murdoch

A resident from Glebe Street, Mr Hamish McTavish, alerted me to the fact that his plum tree had been plundered whilst he slept in his garden shed. He believes Fat Bob and his pal Wullie to be the culprits of this devastating crime. Investigations continue. Must get to the bottom of this as Hamish had promised a punnet o' plums for ma Sunday pudding. Plum crumble it would hae been!

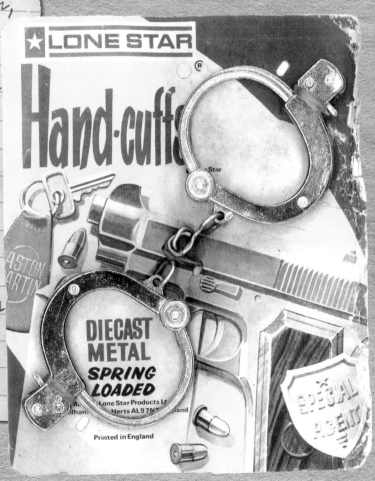

LONE STAR
Hand-cuffs
DIECAST METAL SPRING LOADED
Lone Star Products L... ...ham, Herts AL9 7N... ...land
Printed in England
SPECIAL AGENT

The gang "plundered" this fae P.C. Murdoch's notebook too. He'll no' catch us noo.

21

But he's nae above the law!

22

Ma's sayin's

I cannae understand some o' the things Ma says. I sit there in the kitchen as she's doin' dishes an' bakin' an' stuff, listenin' tae this stuff an' it a' seems awfy daft tae me.

"Wullie - you can talk the hind legs off a donkey."
Weel I went tae the beach wi' Fat Bob an' we followed these donkeys for a day, talkin' the whole time, an' they still gied us a ride wi' a' fower legs.

"A watched pot never boils."

That's plain daft. I've watched pots bilin' for soup on camp fires. They bile every time.

"Wullie - ye cannae burn the candle at both ends."

Aye ye can! Just hold it level, an' sharpen the bottom end wi' a penknife tae get a wick, an' Bob's yer uncle!

"Rome wasn't built in a day."

O' course Rome wisnae built in a day. I've watched the brickies workin' at the Primary School. It would tak' them weeks tae build somethin' the size o' Rome.

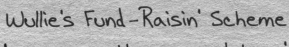

Wullie's Fund-Raisin' Scheme

In summer there are lots o' visitors tae Scotland. Tell them aboot yer ain family history. They may reward ye!

I wonder if Wilbur is in oor lot – perhaps it's American for Wullie. I tellt them a' aboot ma braw ancestors.

> IT'S NO USE, WILBUR! WE CAN'T TRACE ANY SCOTTISH ANCESTORS.
>
> ACH, WHIT A SHAME.

Big Wild Wull, who patrolled the border tae see nae Englishers sneaked ower.

Wee Wullie, who took his conkers tae London. Naebody could beat him so they crowned him Wullie the Conkerer.

Great-Great Uncle Wullie, who went tae America and made friends wi' the Injuns – he taught them tae play the bagpipes an' became Big Chief Sitting Wull.

They liked ma story so much that they gave me a dollar an' a stick o' gum. I couldna let them go hame thinkin' that they had nae Scottish blood.

> HA-HA! I MUST HAVE BEEN GOOD! THEY BELIEVED ME.
>
> WHAT A BOY! I DIDN'T HAVE THE HEART TO SAY WE DIDN'T BELIEVE HIM!

PART 2 - Ma pets an' ither animals

A'body needs tae hae a pet or twa. They keep a laddie company - an' naebody will think ye are mad if ye talk tae a pet rather than tae yersel.

Even P.C. Murdoch has a pet budgie.

Scottish Moose: Smallest member o' the moose family. Bides in hole. Eats cheese. Answers to Jeemy, sometimes.

Puddock: Eats flechs. Bides in jeely jar. Braw for fleggin' Primrose Patterson.

Harry: Originally from the West Highlands. Likes bones. Disnae like cats. Sometimes known as Wull's best friend.

MA FAVOORITE PETS
JEEMY THE MOOSE
HARRY THE WESTIE
JOCKIE THE RABBIT
MA GOLDFISH
MA PUDDOCK
MA BUCKET
MA WORMS

P.C. Murdoch's budgie: Colour: Blue, with copper ring. Favoorite sayings: "Evening a'" and "Now then, whit's a' this?"

But I dinna like it when Ma calls me "her wee pet". I'm a laddie no' an animal an' she should ken that! When ye hae a pet ye've got tae look after it well. Jist remember, as the sayin' goes, "A pet is for life, no' jist for Christmas."

Jeemy

Jeemy is ma moose an' well kent tae ye' a'. We understand each ither, but I had tae work at it.

SQUEAK!

MOUSE MONTHLY

No. 5 MAY

2d

BUILD YOUR VERY OWN MOUSE CAGE
SEE PAGE 6

BAN THE TRAP

...TO MAKE **YOU** CASH!

Mice varieties

There are many different varieties and colours of mouse which can be kept as pets. These have all been developed from the wild house mouse, which has the scientific name of **Mus musculus**. Although the wild mouse is always brown, strains of pet mouse have now been developed which are white, black and piebald.

Mice grow up very quickly, and can begin to breed when only between six and eight weeks of age. Their gestation period (the time between mating and babies being born) is 21 days, and the babies can leave their mother when they are only three weeks old. Mice normally live for only two or three years.

They require very simple cages, but these should not be thin wood, as mice, like all rodents, can soon gnaw a hole and escape. Males often fight among themselves, and the cages have to be frequently cleaned as mice can smell rather strongly.

Keeping mice means hard work
Keeping mice as pets can be a rewarding and fascinating hobby. Many become extremely tame, and a great deal can be learnt from studying their behaviour. However, no pet should be kept without serious thought of what it involves. It is much easier to neglect a small mouse in a cage than a cat or dog, which will soon let you know if it is hungry or wants some exercise.

Fig. 2. Different strains of pet mouse

A mouse, or any other small pet such as a guinea pig, depends entirely on its owner for food and general comfort. This means attention to all its needs every day of the week, and every week of the year.

You should not decide to keep a pet mouse – unless you are prepared to do all the work yourself, although holidays away from home and illness are exceptions when it is useful to be able to rely on parents or friends to help out. This close association with your pet mouse is very important to enable both you and it to get the maximum benefit from your relationship. Frequent handling is of great assistance in the taming of a pet mouse, so long as this does not obviously upset it, and is done in a sensible way.

Keepin' it warm.

How tae haud a moose

Jeemy really likes bein' held – an' I like haudin' him. I wis a bit worried aboot daeing it at first, so here is some guid advice for ye.

How to hold a mouse

It is very important to know how to pick up and handle your mouse in a proper manner. Obviously this handling must not distress your mouse, yet it must be firm enough to prevent it escaping. A mouse can be picked up by its tail without causing it discomfort, and then transferred to your arm or sleeve. If you want to examine the mouse's underside, it can also be picked up by the loose skin behind the neck. This neck skin is called the scruff – and so you can pick up a mouse by the scruff of the neck!

Alternatively, you can grasp a mouse firmly around its chest. This is also the way to pick up pet rats.

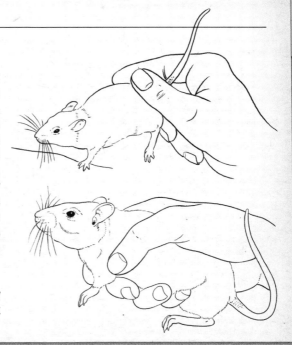

An' he'll need a nice cage tae live in. Ye'll find lots o' ideas in a pet shop, but ye can save some money by makin' yer ain, but dinna mak' it oot o' thin plywood. A moose could eat its way oot! Here's an idea for a cage.

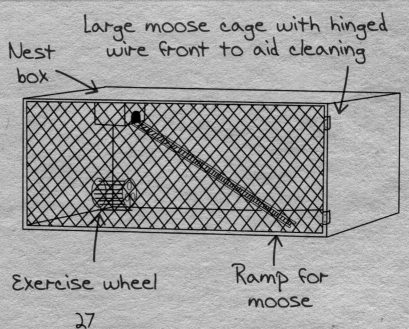

Nest box

Large moose cage with hinged wire front to aid cleaning

Exercise wheel

Ramp for moose

Feeding a moose
Weel, ye a' ken that meece eat cheese.

Wee Jeemy's no' so wee onymore. He weighs aboot half a stane! I'm a bit cross at Jeemy for eatin' my roll an' worried aboot him gettin' fat, so looks like he's needin' tae go on a diet.

"I'm holding Jeemy by the scruff o' his neck"

I took him intae the vet, Dr. Gordon, an' he tellt me tae put him on a special diet. Sorry, Jeemy, but low fat cheese fae now on!

26 MOUSE MONTHLY

Feeding smaller rodents

Feeding the smaller rodents such as mice, rats, hamsters and gerbils is much easier than it was a few years ago, because it is now possible to buy special mouse pellets, which are a good basis for the rations for all of these small pets. These pellets are made from a mixture of cereals, fish meal and dried milk, with extra vitamins added. If good pellets are purchased, mice and rats need no other supplement except water, but, like ourselves, appreciate a little variety. Sunflower seeds are a favourite with all these little animals, and certainly some green food or fruit are very useful and acceptable additions to their diet. If you are unable to buy the pellets, a complete ration could be a mixture of corn, sunflower seed, a small quantity of meat or cheese, some fruit, green food and other vegetables.

WULLIE'S WISDOMS

The best laid schemes o' meece and men aye go astray.

Lookin' efter Jeemy

Jeemy needs tae hae a bath. Use a wee bowl an' add some warm water.

Wullie's tip
Dinna read a book or dae onything else while Jeemy is in the bath. Learn fae ma mistake.

It gave him a sore throat an' an awfy hoarse squeak!

I tried to get ae o' Pa's throat sweets, but he wouldna let me, an' then I asked P.C. Murdoch for some advice.

So I gave Jeemy some castor oil, which he liked!! It worked as weel.

I spoke tae Dr. Gordon, the vet. Tellt him aboot the castor oil and he said it wis clever thinkin', but next time bring Jeemy tae him. Doctor kens best I suppose.

101 THINGS TAE DAE WI' A BUCKET

SQUEAK! SQUEAK! No.8

HIDING JEEMY THE MOUSE WHEN MA'S POSH FRIENDS COME

Harry the Westie

Harry's my best pal. There's somethin' special aboot Westies. They can be stubborn – just like us. They're Scottish o' course and their posh name is The West Highland White Terrier.

I talk tae Harry a lot. I tell him secrets and a'thing. He listens – ye need tae speak kindly but firmly – but dinna shout at a Westie!

An' just cos he's wee, it disnae mean he doesn't need as much exercise as a bigger dug.

A dug takes a lot o' lookin' efter – an when ye get an understandin' there's no better pal than a happy dug.

HARRY – BY WULLIE

Facts: Dogs

The smallest dog breed is the Chihuahua. It weighs less than 2 kg (that's only 4 pounds) and it is 5 in. high at its shoulders.

The tallest dog breed is the Irish wolfhound - 1 metre (39 in.) tall at its shoulder.

The heaviest dog is a St. Bernard weighing about 90 kg.

The Yorkshire terrier can have hair 2 ft long but the Mexican hairless has no hair at all.

Some dogs have pointed ears that stand up. Others have ears that hang down.

Some dogs have very short legs like a Basset hound or a Dachshund, or short legs like a Westie, and some have long legs like a Greyhound.

PETS NEWSLETTER

Make Your Own Dog Dossier

You will need a scrapbook, or notebook, or loose-leaf file of some sort, some pencils, coloured crayons or paints, a rubber, ruler, a tape measure, the use of some bathroom or public scales, and finally look in your local library for books about dogs.

Draw a quick sketch of your dog and arrow the different parts of the body on your drawing. The diagram will give you a guide. Take your dog's measurements. Borrow or buy a tape and measure:
• height from the ground to the top of his shoulder,
• the length of his body from the end of his nose to the end of his tail,
• length of his head from the end of his nose to the top of his head,
• girth—the widest part of his body as near to front as possible. Put these measurements onto your sketch.

Weigh him. If possible, use some bathroom scales at home (but ask your parents first). If you cannot get him to stand on the scales on his own, hold him in your arms and first weigh both of you. Then second, weigh yourself. Take your weight away from the first weight and the difference will be the weight of your dog.

Note the colour of your dog's coat and any distinctive markings he has. Using coloured pencils colour your sketch to show this.

Also indicate in your drawing the length of your dog's coat, and make any other observations that you think are important.

HARRY'S DOSSIER

NAME = Harry   AGE = about 10 LICENCE = not needed
COLLAR = "Harry" c/o Wullie's Hoose, 12" in. (31 cm)
COLOUR = White(ish)

NUMBER O' EYES = 2, dark broon

EYEBROWS = Shaggy

GIRTH – WIDEST PART O' HIS BODY NEAR TAE HIS FRONT LEGS = 20 in. (50cm)

HEIGHT FROM GROUND TO TOP O' SHOULDER = 1 in. (28 cm)

LENGTH O' HIS COAT = aboot 2 in. lang (5 cm)

WEST HIGHLAND TERRIER

NUMBER O' TAILS = 1

NUMBER O' LEGS = 4

LENGTH O' HIS BODY FROM HIS NOSE TAE THE END O' HIS TAIL = Cannae get him tae stand still tae get a proper measurement But his tail is about 5 in. (12cm) lang

WEIGHT: 20 pounds (9 kg.)
NUMBER O' TEETH = 42
FAVOORITE FOOD = raw carrots, mince, cauliflower or peas an' dog treats made wi' beef, chicken, lamb an' rice
HEARING = Harry hears the postie lang afore anyone else, but when he disnae want tae listen tae ye he'll no' hear a single thing ye say.

HARRY'S SIGNATURE

Man's best friend

Throughout long ages man and dog have walked together; for centuries they have hunted side by side, have worked together and played together. The dog has been man's companion for thousands of years and today fulfils all the roles he has played in his history. He works on farms and moorlands and is invaluable to the hunter; he is exalted in the exhibition ring; industries of dog food and biscuit manufacture, kennel building, appliance making and show breeding have grown up around him; many people have made money out of breeding him; many people have written about him; he has been the hero of films; and the central figure of famous paintings; he is the trusted guardian of men's homes and property, but above all this he is the faithful friend and companion of tens of thousands of people, young and old, who love him.

Breeds and types of dog
Dogs are divided into two groups: mongrel or crossbred, and pedigree. Pedigree dogs are further divided into different breeds; these are roughly distinguished by shape or appearance as well as their size, colour and weight. Some of the most popular breeds of dog in this country are Alsatians, Poodles, Retrievers, Cocker Spaniels, Terriers, Boxers, Pekinese and Beagles.

Pedigree or pure bred dogs can be broadly classified into the following five groups:

The sporting terriers: Although differing in size, coat, and markings, all are extremely hardy and courageous. The largest of them are the Airedale and Bull Terrier; among the smallest are the Dandie Dinmont and the West Highland White.

The hunters and chasers: These include the larger sporting breeds such as Foxhounds, the Irish Wolfhound, the Greyhound, the Bloodhound, the Borzoi, the Afghan and the Saluki. Smaller hunters include the Beagle, Basset, Harrier, Dachshund and Whippet.

The gundog breeds: These are well known and include the large family of Spaniels, Setters, Pointers and Retrievers.

Non-sporting breeds: In this group are included the Bulldog, the Sheepdog, the Dalmatian, the St. Bernard, the Mastiff, the Great Dane and the Corgi.

Toy dogs: This group is composed of all the smaller breeds including the Pekinese, the Pomeranian, the Yorkshire Terrier and the King Charles Spaniel.

9

Ye might look tough but Harry wid see ye aff!

THE BEST

32

Where tae keep yer dug

Ma disnae like having Harry sleepin' in the hoose. He now bides in ma shed an' sleeps in an auld comfy chair. Pa says he should stay in a kennel. Mebbe he would build Harry ane like this if he were so minded. Aye, that would be richt!

Make a dog kennel

Before deciding where you are going to place the kennel, remember this following golden rule. The opening should always face away from the prevailing wind, preferably into a hedge or wall, which can then act as a wind-break. However, if this is not possible, build a baffle wall.

You will have to decide what size the kennel should be. Make it so that it is large enough to permit your dog to turn round completely, and stand up normally.

What you will need
You will need tongued and grooved (T&G) boarding to make the two longer sides and the two ends. Estimate the size it needs to be and then work out how much wood you will need. Also buy two pieces of wood for the roof and some roofing felt to cover it. You will also need a saw and a large number of 1¼ in. (30 mm) galvanised nails.

The illustration gives you an idea of the shape of the kennel. The kennel floor, which can be made of wood also, should be raised about 2 in. (50 mm) off the ground.

Construct the kennel in such a way that there are no cracks or

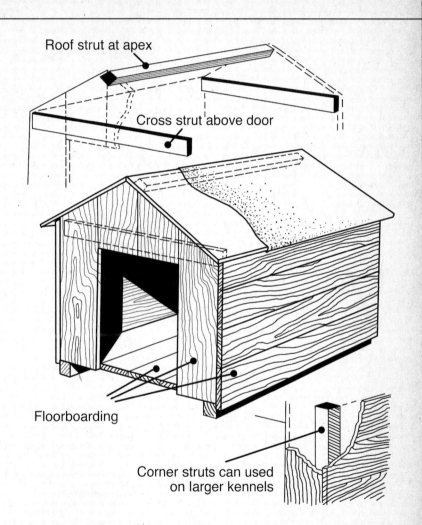

Roof strut at apex

Cross strut above door

Floorboarding

Corner struts can used on larger kennels

joints to permit draughts, either through using tongued and grooved board or by covering the outer surface with roofing felt. You should build the roof so that it has an overhang to prevent rain from getting into the

kennel. The roof must be covered in a waterproof material (such as roofing felt).

Finally place a warm draught-free bed in the kennel for the dog to sleep on.

9

Wullie's Fund-Raisin' Scheme

I had a braw idea. I'd use ma shed tae keep pets in ower the weekend for a modest fee. I wis daein' a roarin' trade.

Wee Eck wis ma last customer – he wanted his flyin' ants looked efter. Soon I had the shed in order.

On the Monday mornin', I went tae check the flyin' ants, an' that's when the trouble began. I lifted the lid an' then bumped ma heid as they came oot so quickly. The shelf collapsed an' a' the animals escaped.

It wis chaos. Never again!!

WULLIE WISDOMS

A fool may earn money, but it tak' a wise heid tae keep it.

34

Wullie's Fund-Raisin' Scheme
The circus wis in town,
an' I came awa' wi' an idea
tae haud oor ain circus wi'
performin' dugs. Tae get the
dugs, I had a dug walkin' day
at the High Field. It cost fowk
sixpence for the day – an' I
would teach the dugs some
tricks an' haud a circus at
the end o' the day.

Wullie's Dug Services

Your dug exorcised by top
profeshnal handlers
This Saturday –
ONLY 6d per dug
The High Field,
fae 9 o'clock.
Get yer dug back
at 5 o'clock.

The dugs did a' kind
o' tricks for me.

But there wis nae show – the dugs a' ran back tae their
owners at the end o' the day, an' I had tae pay back a'body
who came tae see Wullie's Wizard Circus.

35

Ma rabbit is ca'd Jockie. Ma thinks I spend so long lookin' after him that I am beginnin' tae look like a rabbit masel'. That's daft!

I canna believe it! Jockie escaped from his hutch again. I had tae look a' ower the place.

HEY! HAVE ONY O' YOU ANES SEEN MY JOCKIE?

IT'S HOPELESS ASKIN' THEM!

Then I found him near Granpaw Broon's veg patch.

Cheeky wee monkey wis aboot tae help himsel' tae some carrots when I chased him intae wee Andy Drummond's house.

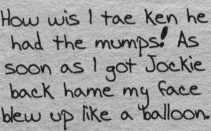

How wis I tae ken he had the mumps! As soon as I got Jockie back hame my face blew up like a balloon.

Ma had tae wrap it in a sheet. Dinna say that I look like Jockie. Ma already has.

As soon as I'm well I'm gonna build Jockie a new hutch!

Make a hutch

With the aid of the diagram, make your own hutch. The dimensions shown are suitable for a rabbit, but they could be rather less if it is meant for a guinea-pig. The larger you can afford to make the hutch the better.

There should be separate doors for both the sleeping quarters and the open part. The floors should be as smooth as possible to make them more easy to keep clean, and the roof should slope backwards and be covered with roofing felt so that the rain will run off. The outside should be painted with some non-poisonous wood preservative, and simple catches should be fitted to the doors, preferably of the kind to which padlocks could be attached if required.

If you have a lawn, rabbits, guinea-pigs and chinchillas enjoy an outside run during the warmer weather. They can be kept outside all night during the summer months, but you should make sure that they are quite safe from wandering cats and dogs, and beware of hungry foxes. Make an enclosure with strong fencing.

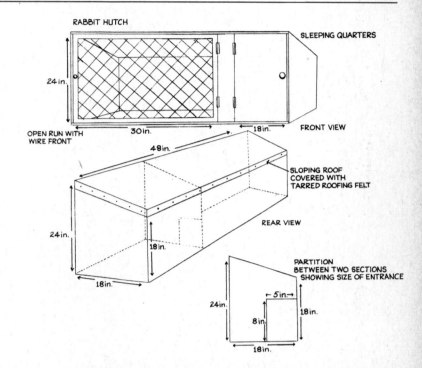

Rabbits

All our different breeds of pet rabbit have developed from the European wild rabbit (*Oryctolagus cuniculus*). Wild rabbits can be a serious pest to the gardener and the farmer because of the large amount of plants (including flowers, vegetables and other agricultural crops) they eat.

The domestic breed of rabbit were primarily produced either for food or for their pelts or skins, and now many varieties are well established.

Rabbits are naturally docile creatures, which live for several years. They require quite a large cage or hutch, and, ideally, outside runs in summer. Although they are easy to feed, they have rather large appetites and need constant attention.

They are usually ready to breed when 6-8 months old, and have a gestation period of 31 days. Babies can be taken from the mother, or doe, when 8 weeks old.

Fig. 6. *Angora (top) and Dutch rabbits*

Cats

Cats dinna appear much around oor hoose.
Ma's no' keen, and it's no' easy tae hae a pet moose, a goldfish and a dug and hae a cat as well and keep the peace.

Black cats seem tae be the maist interestin'. P.C. Murdoch says that in Scotland, if a black cat crosses yer path it is meant tae be a sign o' guid things tae come, and if ye get hame tae a strange black cat sittin' on yer doorstep it means guid luck. Strange, but fowk think the opposite in ither countries. Ancient Egyptians used tae think that the rays o' the sun were kept in a cat's eyes at nicht tae keep them safe.

Black cats hae supernatural powers and maist proper witches, at Halloween will hae their black cat, ridin' on a broomstick, and witches could change intae cats, up tae nine times. Maybe that's why cats hae nine lives.

...but watch oot for cats who like goldfish fingers!

Jeemy wis supposed tae be oor mascot at the fitba' but it turned oot that the ither lot had a black cat for their mascot, so that wis a bit o' a disaster. Jeemy is quick aff the mark though!

Cats can keep ye aff yer sleep! Whit a noise – an a' because the cat thocht I'd still hae the milk I'd been deliverin' in the morn!

CAT'S EYES

CAT'S EYES are reflective road safety aids set into the road surface, invented by Percy Shaw from Halifax, in England in 1933. Cat's Eyes are effective at night in difficult driving conditions, such as mist and fog and are designed to be resistant to damage by snow ploughs.

Originally made with two sets of reflective glass balls, like marbles, set into a rubber mould within a metal frame, with one set of eyes showing in each direction from a central position in the road.

A one-ended pair is used in other colours for different purposes visible to traffic going in one direction.

White Cat's Eyes are used to mark the centre of a road particularly where there is no standard street lighting, and are used to mark different lanes and on "double-white lines" (no overtaking).

● Red Cat's Eyes mark the hard shoulder of dual carriageways and motorways.
● Amber / Orange Cat's Eyes mark an edge of a central reservation (median).
● Green Cat's Eyes mark slip roads at junctions
● Blue Cat's Eyes mark police slip roads.

This is the best kind o' cat!

POETRY HAMEWORK - OOR ANIMAL FRIENDS

The cuddy is a braw, braw lad,
Sure it's a noble beast.
But dinna go ower near the brute,
He'll eat yer jeely piece!

The willing horse is aye worked tae death.

The peeky knees is a poor wee sowel,
It widna harm a flea.
But though the fleas are safe enough,
Jings! I'm no' safe, no' me!

The coo, the coo, the bonny coo,
It's better than a dug,
Until it flicks its muckle tail
And skelps ye ower the lug!

Poetry gies me a BUZZ!

So gie me Paddy every time,
Paddy my wee frog.
He's better than a horse or coo
Or ony type o' dog!

(Sorry Harry –
I didna mean it
– I just couldna
think o' onthing
tae rhyme wi'
frog.)

D+

Come and see
me about this
poor work.

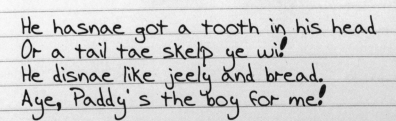

He hasnae got a tooth in his head
Or a tail tae skelp ye wi'!
He disnae like jeely and bread.
Aye, Paddy's the boy for me!

Tadpoles an' puddocks

It's a rare treat each spring tae see frogspawn change intae tadpoles an' tadpoles change intae puddocks. I'm a dab hand at catchin' tadpoles wi' ma net...

THIS IS GOOD FUN! IT'S A LANG TIME SINCE I WENT CATCHIN' TADPOLES.

...an' takin' them back tae ma shed in a jar.

Here's a picture o' the changes fae frogspawn tae a big tadpole - whit a frownin' face!

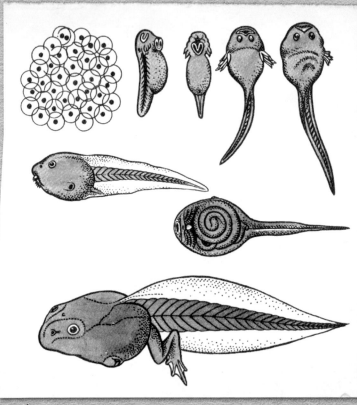

I find puddocks near the woods an' in some o' the bigger gairdens roond aboot. They like puddles tae, an' ponds o' course. Ye can hear the male frogs croakin' - a low purring sound - but ye've got tae listen carefully.

You'll hear an' see them mair at night. In the winter they hibernate in compost heaps, under stones an' logs, or in the water under piles o' mud an' rottin' leaves.

Puddocks are amfibians. Tae improve yer educashun, here's mair aboot them an' reptiles.

36   Nature World   SUMMER SPECIAL

Introducing reptiles and amphibians

The obvious difference between the amphibians and the reptiles lies in their development. Amphibians grow from an egg into a tadpole which is a totally different shape to the adult animal, as well as breathing and swimming in a different way. After a time the tadpole changes into a small copy of the adult and then grows larger. This change in growing up is called metamorphosis (a Greek term meaning 'change of form').

How to identify amphibians

The frog has a smooth, soft skin, although in the breeding season it is slightly roughened by small warts and has webs between all the toes of the hind feet except for the fourth toe. Its colour varies and it grows up to 3¾ in. (95 mm) long.

The toad which is up to 3½ in. (90 mm) long has a coarse, warty skin, with the largest of the warts having a central spine. The colouring is varied, and generally fits in with the surroundings in which it is living.

Puddocks dinnae eat durin' the breedin' season but when they are hungry they eat insects, snails, slugs an' worms, that they catch wi' their long, sticky tongues.

How to identify reptiles

The reptiles are seasonal in their appearance, spending much of the winter in hibernation.

The ***slow-worm*** is a legless lizard with small, smooth scales, giving it a highly polished look. Colour variable, but usually plain on the back and sides. It grows to 18 in. (450 mm) long.

The ***sand lizard*** is a typical lizard which grows to 7½ in. (190 mm) long. Light brown or greyish, with three rows of dark brown or black blotches each with a central white dot. The males also have bright green sides.

The ***viviparous lizard*** is the most common lizard in Britain. It has a dark streak down its back, and one each side, which may be broken into blotches, but they do not have white centres. The background colour is dark, but very variable, and its length is almost the same as the sand lizard.

The ***ringed*** or ***grass-snake*** is olive-green or brown with black flecks along the sides, a white or yellow upper lip with dark bars. The ring around the neck is usually yellow, but can be orange or pinkish, with two triangular blackish patches on the neck. This snake can grow up to 69 in. (1.75 m) long.

The ***smooth snake*** is grey or light brown above, with a series of small dark spots along its back and sides. It is a long thin snake, 25 in. (630 mm) fully grown, with its head only a little wider than its body.

The ***adder*** is the only British snake whose bite is poisonous. It is a rather thick-set snake by comparison with the others, with a short tail and a head distinctly wider than its 'neck'. In ground colouring it is variable, and ranges from grey to dark brown, but it always has a black zigzag marking down the centre of its back. It grows to 25 in. (630 mm) long.

WULLIE'S WISDOMS

Once bitten, twice shy.

Sand lizard

Grass snake

Smooth snake

Slow-worm

Worms

Worms are not so much pets
as useful craiters tae look
after an' sell (as well as
annoyin' Ma).

No. 21 STORE WORMS FOR FISHIN'

Ma worm catchin' tips

Lay a piece o' damp cardboard
down overnight in the gairden.
Wake up early enuff in the mornin' tae find
lots o' worms hidin' under it.

Worms can be slippery wee beasties.
Rub sand intae yer fingertips tae mak' it
easier tae haud them.

Keep them fresh for fishin' the next day by
puttin' them in an auld ice-cream box full o'
dirt. Then put the box in the fridge (dinna
tell Ma).   Ma found oot aboot the
                worms. Dinna try tae put
                worms in the fridge - it's
                nae worth the trouble!

If ye need worms fast, always hae a big
stick or wooden stake half buried in the
gairden, rub a lang piece o' metal on the
upright top o' the stake tae frighten the
worms oot o' the ground.

Never cut a worm in twa. It'll no' gie ye
twa worms, jist a deid worm an' it's awfy
cruel too.

The BIGGEST ⟶
worm I ever found

BAIT ON YOUR HOOK

by Big Hank (Caster) Carter Junior - The Angler's Angler

WORMS

There are many kinds of worms, but as far as I am concerned, there are just three types - big worms, small worms and middle-sized ones.

My favourites are lobworms. The Americans call these worms 'night-crawlers', owing to their habit of crawling out of their holes on damp, calm nights. If you tread softly on a close-cropped lawn with a torch you will see the worms lying full length on the grass. They look so easy to catch – try to pick one up and see what happens . . . you will be surprised at the speed with which a worm can move.

You can, though, trap them if you are quick and quiet. Place a finger across the worm's body near where its tail disappears down its hole. Then take hold of the worm between the fingers, and pull gently but firmly. Gradually the worm will come free. Do not pull too hard, or it will break. Never keep broken worms. They quickly turn foul, and will kill all the others in your bait box.

Keep the live worms in a plastic or wooden bait box with some damp (but not wet) earth. Some people prefer moss, others recommend damp sacking. Try them for yourself, and see which gives you the healthiest worms. A golden rule is to check your worm supply every day, and throw any dead or sick-looking ones away. If you do not, they will quickly affect the others, and you will lose the lot.

Aye weel - he might be the Angler's Angler but he disnae ken as much aboot worms as I dae!

The leaky bucket trick
Ever seen a seagull dance? When they tap their feet on the ground. Pa tellt me they dae that tae trick the worms intae believin' it's rainin'. This gave me an idea.

1. Get yer auldest bucket an' put some holes in the bottom. Not too many though (Pa did it for me while I supervised, jist as it should be!)
2. Hang a piece o' string between twa trees, or anything similar, in the back gairden.
3. Attach the bucket tae the string so it's hangin' ower some grass.
4. Fill the bucket wi' water an' it will dribble oot the holes like rain.
5. Collect a' the worms that come oot the ground.

46

Wullie's Fund-Raisin' Scheme

Fishermen are a' after worms, but they never pay mair than a penny a dozen. Now it's aff tae dig I go.

A' ma work wasted. Mebbe a cat will help keep the birds awa'!

Nae guid, ither! Then I had an idea.

Soon I had a bucket full an' took them aff tae the fisherman.

How did I dae it? Wi' the help o' a bulldozer an' a digger at the buildin' site!

Whit a braw scheme!

Mair o' Ma's sayin's

"Paddle your own canoe."

Weel, who else is gonnae paddle it? There's only room for ae person!

"Don't shut the stable door after the horse has bolted."

If the horse bolted, why would it need shut?

"Don't put a' your eggs in one basket."

Disnae matter if they're hard biled!

"Don't make a mountain out of a molehill."

How could a'body make a mountain fae a wee pile o' earth? You'd need piles o' piles!

"The best things come in small packages."

Now just think aboot this. Christmas presents . . . I think big is best!

↑ Jist look at that cartie.
The bestest ever.

A'body needs a cartie. It's the bestest fun ye can hae. I found these plans in ae o' Pa's magazines, an' it tells ye how tae build a real smart cartie. But ye dinna hae tae build it fae new. See what ye can find aroond tae build it for free. That's whit I dae.

101
THINGS
TAE DAE
WI' A
BUCKET

No. 5
CRASH HELMET FOR
CART RACING

MAKE A CARTIE

For the chassis you will need a 36 in. (900 mm) length of hardwood, about 6 x 1½ in. (150 x 38 mm) and two 24 in. (600 mm) lengths of 3 x 1 in. (75 x 25 mm) hardwood.

1. One of the 24 in. lengths is secured to the main member about 6 in. (150 mm) in from one end to form the rear axle beam. Use three or four bolts for fastening the two pieces together. Do not rely on woodscrews or nails.

2. The front axle beam is assembled on a single bolt, at least ½ in. (12.5 mm) diameter, with the hole in the main member slightly larger than the bolt. This allows the bolt to pivot in this hole so that the front axle beam can move for steering. Note particularly how this assembly is made:
• The bolt head comes at the top, with a large flat metal washer underneath it.
• Sandwiched between the main member and the axle beam is a 3 in. (75 mm) diameter circle cut from ¼ in. (6 mm) ply which acts as a bearing washer.
• On the underside of the axle beam first there is another flat metal washer.
• This is followed by two nuts to hold the bolt in place. Tighten up the first nut until there is enough slack for the axle beam to pivot easily. Then tighten the second nut up against the first. This will lock the nuts in position.

3. Wheels and axles are always a bit of a problem. It is really a case of seeing what you can find somewhere — preferably small pram wheels or pushchair wheels, complete with their original axles. These can then be fastened to the bottom of the axle beams by means of a couple of steel plates each drilled with four holes and held in place with bolts or screws. It is always best to use complete wheel and

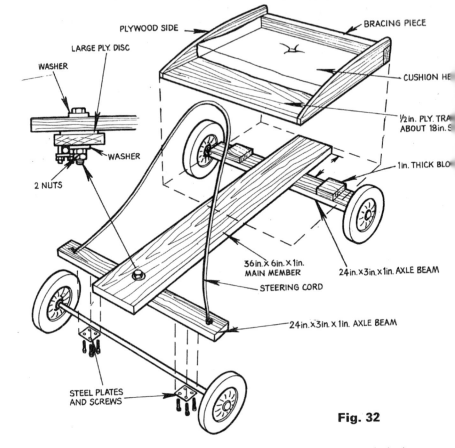

PLYWOOD SIDE
LARGE PLY. DISC
WASHER
2 NUTS
WASHER
BRACING PIECE
CUSHION HE[...]
½ in. PLY. TRA[...] ABOUT 18 in. S[...]
1 in. THICK BLO[...]
36 in. X 6 in. X 1 in. MAIN MEMBER
24 in. X 3 in. X 1 in. AXLE BEAM
STEERING CORD
24 in. X 3 in. X 1 in. AXLE BEAM
STEEL PLATES AND SCREWS

Fig. 32

axle units, if you can. The length of the axle beams can always be adjusted to suit.

4. The body needs to be nothing more than a shallow tray shape, with the bottom and sides cut from 3/8 in. (9 mm) or 1/2 in. (12 mm) ply. The base of the tray should be around 18 in. (450 mm) square. A piece of stripwood secured across the back will stiffen the assembly, and you can always add a cushion for a more comfortable seat.

5. The tray is simply screwed down on to the main frame. Additional small blocks should be glued or screwed to the rear axle beam to support the width of the

tray, screwing down through the bottom of the tray into these blocks.

6. Give the whole job a smart paint finish.

7. Do not forget to add the steering lines. These are simply a loop of rope taken through holes bored near the outer ends of the front axle beam. Adjust the length of loop so that you can hold it comfortably when seated. Your feet should also normally rest on the front axle beam, one each side, and can be used to assist steering. For braking dig your heels into the ground. Hard on shoe leather—but effective.

New wheels for ma cartie

It's nae easy tae find the pairts ye need. Ma back wheels were a' buckled. How could I get the cartie repaired in time for the 'Soapbox Derby'?

The scrapyard had nae auld wheels.

Have you ever wondered why a cartie race is called a 'Soapbox Derby'?

In times past soap was sent from the factory to the shops in large wooden boxes (this was at a time before cardboard boxes). Once the shopkeeper had taken out the packets of soap, there was an empty wooden box to get rid of. It wasn't long before wheels were added to the discarded boxes and the cartie was born.

As for 'Derby', well that name is taken from the famous horse race that has been run every year since 1780 at Epsom Downs, just to the south of London. It was named after the Earl of Derby, a great racing enthusiast who had a house nearby.

The Americans take soapbox derby racing really quite seriously, and a world championship has been held every year since 1934 at Akron in Ohio. There are many different classes, and races take place over a whole week. The streamlined machines are a long way from a traditional cartie!

Recently there has been an annual Cartie Challenge run down the hill from the Creel Inn to the harbour at Catterline in Kincardineshire while, since 2009, there has been a Cairngorm Soapbox Extreme. The course is over 2 miles long and descends over 680 ft. with an expected maximum speed of 63 mph. A streamlined Bentley soapbox made by apprentices at the car manufacturer, is one of the challengers.

Mrs Megaton wis happy for me tae push her bairn, Davie, in the pram. Ma pals gave me a lot o' grief.

Mair aboot this ower the page. ⟶

At last I got the pram an' Davie back tae ma shed an' then the work really began.

I took a set o' wheels aff the pram an' fixed them tae ma cartie. Pram wheels are the dab for carties. Now it wis time tae show the lads wha's the big Jessie.

Davie an' me won o' course, an', like a guid team, we shared the prize. That wis a braw race!

(But I had to pit the wheels back on the pram.)

Auchenshoogle Soapbox Derby 35th Annual Championship WINNER Wullie

52

There are a' kinds o' ways a cartie can look. Here are a few designs I came up wi'.

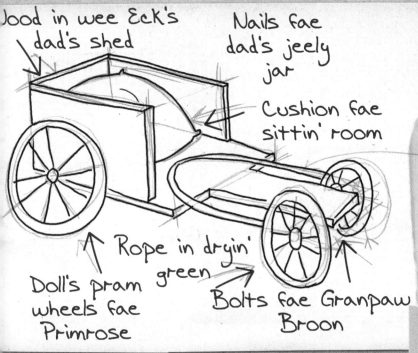

Wood in wee Eck's dad's shed

Nails fae dad's jeely jar

Cushion fae sittin' room

Rope in dryin' green

Doll's pram wheels fae Primrose

Bolts fae Granpaw Broon

Mak' yer ain racing car!

If ye dinna fancy a plain cartie, ye could try a smarter car. Me an' Fat Bob had a go at buildin' ane. It's no' as easy as we hoped tae mak' a quick bob or twa.

There wis lots o' odd bits o' wood in ma gairden, an' we thocht we could mak' somethin' wi' them. First, we tried tae mak' a bit o' furniture. We decided tae mak' a sideboard, worth aboot fifteen pound we wis sure. So we worked hard at it an' made a grand job o' it. I wis pleased wi' the back I had done, until:

So we hae tae tak' the sideboard tae pieces and thocht again. This time we thocht we would mak' somethin' we were guid at like a cartie, so we started tae mak' somethin' special.

It wis a beauty an' soon we had interest. ⟶

BUT...

CARTIE BAN

Following complaints from the local residents and from the police, in the form of that great servant of the force, PC Murdoch, the council discussed the nuisance caused by carties speeding down Dandery Brae

Councillor McStuffy said that many of his constituents were afraid to go out of their houses because of irresponsible boys in their carties speeding down the road. Only Councillor Soutar spoke in favour of boys enjoying cartie racing, an activity he partook of in his younger days.

The Council has therefore decided that Dandery Brae shall become a 'no cartie area'. Signs will shortly be erected. Meanwhile PC Murdoch will increase his attendance in this area to stop speeding carties.

Other local news in brief

A sad day for a' cartie lovers!

AUCHENSHOOGLE POLICE STATION
DATE ... *Friday 3rd* ...
POLICE CONSTABLE ... *Murdoch* ...

I was progressing along Dandery Brae when I heard a great commotion behind me. Turning around I observed three juveniles coming down the road at speed in their carties. I put out my hand to signal to them to stop. However, the carties had no brakes and could not slow down. I tried to pursue them but they were too fast for me. I identified two of the drivers as William and Bob and shall reprimand them. For the safety of residents, I shall suggest that this area becomes a 'cartie-free' zone.

Mair haste, less speed!

I suppose some day I'll be happier with a car than a cartie. Here are some really great auld cars - as well as some that look as though I had invented them!

Even smart horses were said to be fooled by Uriah Smith's automobile that had a horse's head up front

With eight wheels to smooth the bumps, this weird car was called the Octoauto

If you wanted to be a back-seat driver, you bought the 1913 Dutc

Ye'd aye be oot o' pocket buyin' tyres for this monste mobile.

old buggy? With a replace the horse, reins for steering

I thought ma cartie could be a
guid money makin' venture . . .

Ma sledge

Sledges are great in the sna'. Once a lang time past, we didnae ken aboot wheels an' sleds were used when there wasnae any sna'. Can ye imagine that! Look how the Pharaoh o' Egypt moved aboot. I wouldna' fancy bein' ane o' his slaves pullin' him aroond.

Slowly emerging from the age of the stone tool, our ancestors ceased to rely solely on hunting for their food and started to grow it. Farming, the first 'industry', was founded and communities developed around it. Two great areas of invention, which must form the backbone of this book, were opened up: Transport and Communication

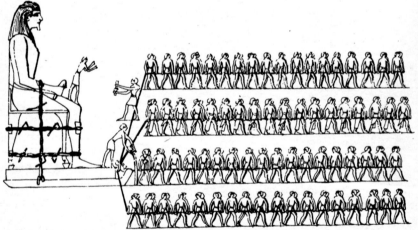

Fig. 4. *The Egyptian mode of transport before the adoption of the wheel*

I showed this tae Ma and she tellt me tae look again at the picture – that's not the Pharoah but a great big statue o' him they are pullin'. Still looks like hard work.

I did try tae mak' ma sledge work when there wisnae any sna'. Fixin' roller skates tae the bottom did well but when I tried chair castors I lost control and hit a lamp post. Never again.

Oh, sledge
Here ye are waitin' tae gie me a hurl,
But ye canna, 'cos there's nae sna'!

When it sna's ye dinnae need tae hae a sledge – ye can use a tin tray, plastic bags, table tops and hunners o' ither things. Dinnae tell P.C. Murdoch but I even saw twa policemen usin' their riot shields!

A sledge is best, an' ye can mak' yer ain.

1. Mak' twa runners 3 ft. (900 mm) lang, 6 in. (150 mm) tall. Mind an' roond aff the front end or it'll no' go!

2. Mak' a hole near the end tae thread the rope through.

3. 8 slats o' wood 18 in. (450 mm) lang, 4 1/2 in (115 mm) wide, an' 1 in. (25 mm) thick. Screw slats tae runners wi' twa screws at each end o' each slat.

4. Fit three cross braces tae mak' the sledge rigid. Screw tae runners and tae the bottom o' the slats.

5. Add metal strips tae the bottom o' the runners. Aluminium strips are the easiest tae fix.

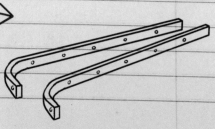

A cartie land-cruiser

It's been awfy windy an' this gave me an idea. Whit would happen if I fixed a sail tae ma cartie? I wouldna just hae tae go doonhill, an' I could pretend tae be a pirate ship or a man o' war or the Cutty Sark. Soon I had ma sail rigged an' aff I went.

It wisnae easy tae steer an' control.

Mebbe sailin' a boat is mair difficult than it looks.

I found this auld book o' Pa's that had advice aboot sailing, but that only made things worse as I couldna understand it, what wi' words like "tacking", "luffing", "gyring" an' the like. Aboot the only things I understood were:

"When alone in a boat don't attempt to row and sail at the same time."

"Give big ships, especially steamers, a wide berth."

FIG. 99.—This illustration shows the distinctive rigs of six classes of sailing ships. Every amateur yachtsman should be able to name the rig of a ship under sail.

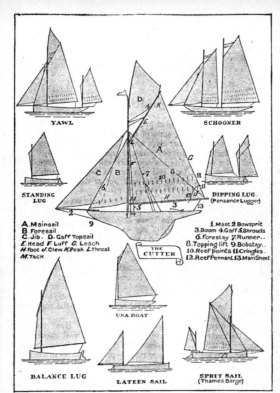

FIG. 95.—Showing various kinds of rigs, and (in centre) naming parts of sails, ropes, etc.
194

From Pa's auld book.

But I didnae need a book tae tell me this.
Jist think how fast a full-rigged cartie could move.

PART 4 - Makin' models an' things

We laddies aye want tae mak' models - boats, aeroplanes, tanks an' the like. Here are some ideas for models tae mak' for fun an' some that ye can mebbe mak' some money wi'.

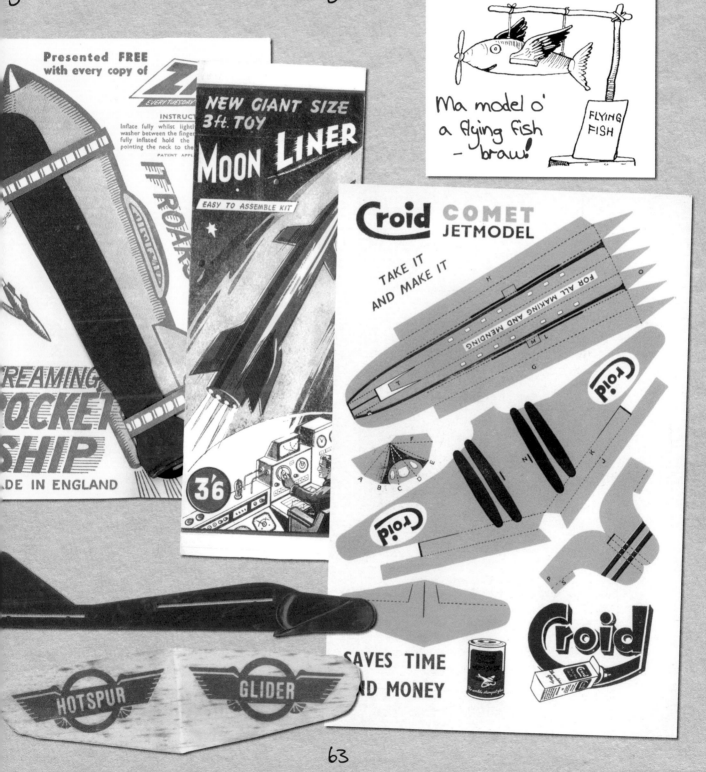

Ma model o' a flying fish - braw!

FLYING FISH

Presented FREE with every copy of ZI...
EVERY TUESDAY

INSTRUCT...
Inflate fully whilst lightl... washer between the finger... fully inflated hold the... pointing the neck to the...
PATENT APPL...

STREAMING ROCKET SHIP
...DE IN ENGLAND

NEW GIANT SIZE 3ft. TOY
Moon LINER
EASY TO ASSEMBLE KIT
3'6

Croid COMET JETMODEL
TAKE IT AND MAKE IT
FOR ALL MAKING AND MENDING
Croid
Croid
Croid
SAVES TIME ...ND MONEY

HOTSPUR GLIDER

Rafts an' boats

I've aye wanted tae sail a raft doon a river, but I couldna believe that some fowk had sailed a raft across the Pacific Ocean! It wis ca'd the Kon-Tki Expedition. I canna wait tae make a model o' the raft.

The Kon-Tiki Expedition

MAN'S FIRST 'boat' was a log on which he sat astride. Men living in Ecuador, in South America, were lucky. They had balsa trees growing all around them. Balsa is the lightest of woods, so a balsa log floats better than any other log. By lashing balsa logs together in the form of a raft the made seaworthy craft more than three thousand years ago. In 194 the Norwegian, Thor Heyerdahl, wanted to test the theory that people from South America coul have settled the Pacific islands. To do this he planned to build a raft out of balsa wood and sail it across the Pacific. The raft was built from nine 2 ft. thick balsa log which were lashed together and t balsa wood cross beams. The dec was made from plaited bamboo and a bamboo hut was built in th middle of the deck. The raft was completed with a mast and sails and a long steering oar.

It was named Kon-Tiki after the creator god who created the world before the Incas and who finally disappeared by walking over the Pacific Ocean. The raft left the coast of Peru on 28 April 1947 with a crew of six, including Heyerdahl, and sailed for 101 day until it landed on a coral reef at Raroia in the Tuamoto Islands, a journey of 4,300 miles. Some thought the balsawood would become waterlogged and so coul not survive a long sea trip. Other thought that there would not be enough food that could be caugh on the way, but there turned ou to be plenty of seafood – flying fish and small squid even arrived unassisted on the raft's deck. The journey showed that people from South America could have colonized the Pacific islands, a theory that was not supported b academics at that time.

SEPTEMBER 21, 1961 — **WOODWORKING WEEKLY**

Make a Kon-Tiki raft

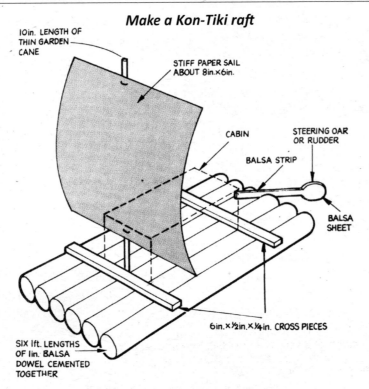

1 Buy two 36 in. (900 mm) lengths of 1 in. (25 mm) diameter balsa dowel, and a 36 in. (900 mm) length of ½ x ¼ in. (12.5 x 6.5 mm) balsa strip from your local model shop. (If you cannot get balsa dowel of this size, buy ¾ in. (19 mm) square balsa strip and round off the edges to a 'log' shape.)
2. Cut the dowel into 1 ft. (300 mm) lengths and cement these together in the shape of a raft.
3. Add the ½ x ¼ in. (12.5 x 6.5 mm) cross pieces to strengthen, and a 10 in. (250 mm) length of garden cane for a mast.
4. Cut a sail from stiff paper and fit as shown. You can make up a 'box' from balsa sheet to act as a shelter, and add a rudder, as shown in the diagram, to make a model of the original Kon-Tiki raft.

You will find that this raft will sail well on any pond or stretch of open water. It will sail only downwind, of course, but it will never sink, or turn over, even if it is rough. Like the ancient Kon-Tiki raft, it is very seaworthy.

Here are two more projects, both using the ideas that went into making the Kon-Tiki raft.

Make a catamaran

Although it may be unsinkable it is very slow since it has to push its way through the water. On the other hand, it owes much of its safety to the fact that it is very wide and difficult to tip over. Over two thousand years ago, somebody in the Southern Seas had the bright idea of combining a slender shape which cuts its way through the water with the width of a raft by joining two shaped logs together with long struts. That was the first catamaran.

The diagram shows how to make a simple model catamaran.

1 Shape the two hulls from 1½ in. (40 mm) square balsa.

2. Fit the same size mast and sail as the Kon-Tiki raft. It will be faster and sail more broadside to the wind, if the sail is fastened at an angle.

If the weather is breezy you will also discover that although the catamaran is faster, it is not as safe as the raft. It can get tipped over in a gust.

Make a trimaran

To avoid being tipped over the trimaran was developed, This uses a long, slender central hull with two smaller hulls or out-rigged floats mounted on cross braces. The diagram shows the construction of a model trimaran using similar parts to the two previous models.

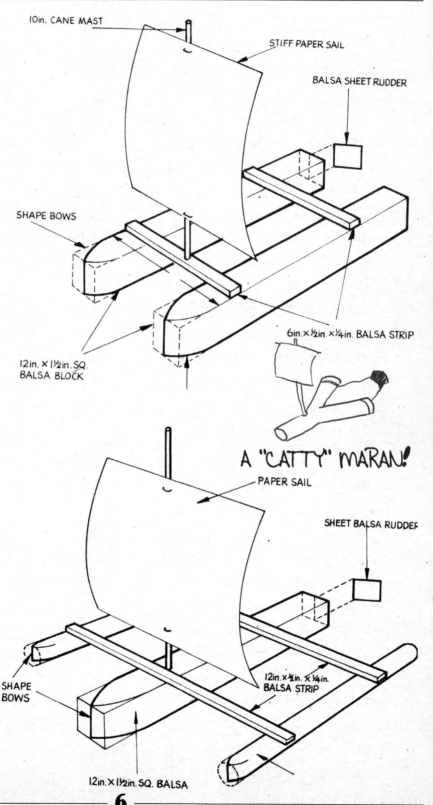

10in. CANE MAST

STIFF PAPER SAIL

BALSA SHEET RUDDER

SHAPE BOWS

6in. × ½in. × ¼in. BALSA STRIP

12in. × 1½in. SQ. BALSA BLOCK

A "CATTY" MARAN!

PAPER SAIL

SHEET BALSA RUDDER

12in. × ¼in. × ¼in. BALSA STRIP

SHAPE BOWS

12in. × 1½in. SQ. BALSA

6

Sailin' boats

Ae day when I wis roller-skatin' alang, Jock, the auld sailor, hollered tae me: "Here Wullie, I've made somethin' for ye."

I picked the boat up an' roller-skated aff tae the park pond tae sail it. It wis windy an' it blew intae the sails as I rollered alang. I fair gave P.C. Murdoch a shock!

But I couldna stop! The boat's got nae brakes and I wis feart o' bein' shipwrecked! It wis awfy choppy sailin' ower cobbles. At last I made it safely tae the park, an' then it wis doon hill tae the pond.

But is wisnae a sea-lic It wis only a dug. I pulle her on board an' starte tae tak' her back tae her maw. She wouldna haud still an' fair wrecke ma sailin' boat. Still, it c worked oot weel in the end.

Here are some ideas for mak' a sailin' boat. Nae danger o' a soakin' wi' this model boat.

SEPTEMBER 28, 1961   **WOODWORKING WEEKLY**

101
THINGS
TAE DAE
WI' A
BUCKET

No. 25

A BOAT FOR WEE ECK.
(STILL TO BE TESTED)

Sailing boat

A model sailing boat is restricted as to the shape of the hull, and the way it can be rigged if it is to sail properly.

The hull shape is usually more curved than a power boat. The side view of the hull is more curved, too, but the smaller the length the more straight 'up and down' the bow and stern lines usually are. This is to get a maximum waterline length. The longer the waterline length, usually, the more sail the yacht can carry and the better it will perform. Since yachts carry a fairly tall mast and sails, the ballast weight is fitted at the bottom of a keel extending from the bottom of the hull. You could not fit enough ballast directly to the bottom of the hull to make a model yacht stable enough under sail. All model yachts, therefore, must have what is called deep keel type hulls.

For the same reason, if you make a scale model of a sailing boat which is not a deep keel type, it will not sail properly. It will lie over on its side in even a slight breeze. The only way to make such a model sail is to fit it with a deep keel with ballast weight at the bottom.

Start modestly

Suitable proportions for a model yacht are shown in the diagram. These hold good for models from about 18 in. (450 mm) long up to 36 in. (900 mm). For a starter, a model yacht of about 24 in. (600 mm) length is about the best.

WATER LINE

BALLAST WEIGHT   RUDDER

TOTAL DEPTH ABOUT ⅓ LENGTH

MAST POSITION

⅓ LENGTH

7

Model yacht hulls are usually of round bilge type. They can be made by shaping and hollowing out a solid block of balsa—but that is an expensive method and not very satisfactory.

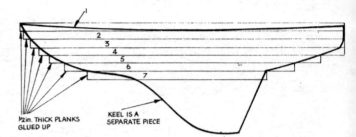

Plank by plank
Another method you can use is bread-and-butter construction, shown here. The hull is made up from a series of flat planks glued together. Each plank is cut to approximate shape, and all but the bottom one or two planks are also cut out in the centre (wood cut out from the top one or two planks will make the bottom two planks). The whole series of shaped planks are then glued up together, ready for finishing by carving. The amount of carving required is fairly small—just blending the planks together into a smooth curve on the outside, and smoothing off the inside.

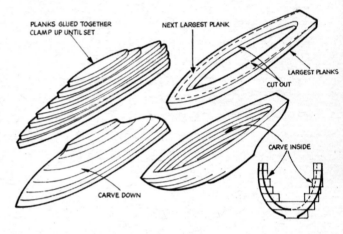

Balsa is quite satisfactory for the planks in a bread-and-butter hull up to 24 in. (600 mm) in length. It is very easy to carve and, being a very light wood, the walls can be left fairly thick. This will ensure that they are strong enough. For a larger hull, you would need to use a stronger wood for the planks, such as obechi. Carving will then be much harder, and you will have to use a plane and gouges as well as a knife.

The vertical keel piece, which fastens to the bottom of the hull, must always be made in strong wood—such as marine ply. This should be slotted and well glued into the hull bottom, making sure that there are no leaks. Another important thing is to get the keel lined up dead straight with the hull.

Cut your own sails

Sails can be cut from polythene sheet. Cut them carefully to the required shape with scissors.

Masts and spars should be of hardwood strip. A simple way of fitting the sails is shown in the diagram. The mast and main boom are each made from two pieces of strip, glued together sandwiching the edge of the sail between them. The smaller foresail has just the boom fitted in this way.

The mast can then fit into a small block called the step, glued to the deck and held in position by a forestay and backstay, and two shrouds, as shown. Use strong thread for the rigging lines, fitted with bowsies so that the length of each line can be adjusted to hold the mast upright and tightly down in the step.

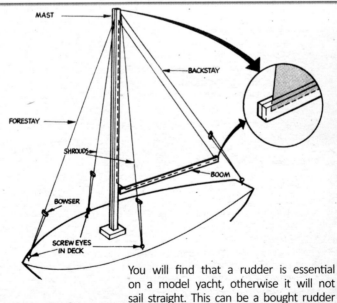

You will find that a rudder is essential on a model yacht, otherwise it will not sail straight. This can be a bought rudder assembly, fitted through the stern end of the hull.

Now ye hae a boat that's ready for a sai on the nearest pond!

Wullie's Fund-Raisin' Scheme

If ye need some cash for yer next model, try penting walls insteaad o' models. I like tae get as much help as I can – then I can dae less!

Ma wanted me oot o' the hoose when the penter came tae stipple the kitchen.

But whit dae ye need a penter for – Wee Jeanne wi' her muddy tennis ba' made a braw stipple.

I had an idea. Soon we wis at work – me, Soapy an' Fat Bob.

THAT'LL DAE! MOVE THE STEP-LADDER ALANG AN' DAE ANITHER BIT.

Then I had an even better idea!

SLAP

WAG

SLAP

THE DOGS TAILS ARE COVERED WI' DISTEMPER, AN' WHEN THEY SEE THE BONES THEY WAG THEIR TAILS AND SLAP THEM AGAINST THE WALL!

OH, JINGS! HERE'S THE MONEY.

The penter even paid me for ma secret! So jist remember it's brains that count if ye want tae mak' some money.

Model Fliers

I like flyin' a kite an' those wee balsa wood gliders that come in a packet. It canna be that bad tae mak' a flier. Specky Spence tellt me he used a 'proper plan'.

Jings, I thocht I could mak' a better flier wi' ma eyes shut. Specky would hae none o' that: "Right, we'll see! You make yours tonight and we'll meet in the park tomorrow tae see who built the best flier - and remember that you've got tae use the plan!"

Build Your Own Glider: Instructions

A balsa glider has to be a reasonable size—with a 10 in. (250 mm) wing-span at least.

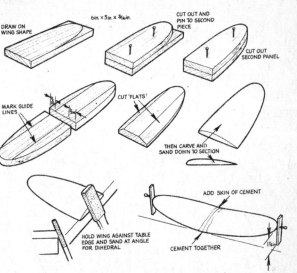

Wings

Use two pieces of 3 in. x 3/16 in. (75 mm x 5 mm) sheet balsa, each 6 in. (150 mm) long. You will have to buy a 24 in. (600 mm) or 36 in. (900 mm) length of sheet from a model shop and cut off these lengths. Choose the lightest sheet of balsa you can find.

1. First, draw a good wing shape on one of the 6 in. (150 mm) pieces and cut it out with a modelling knife.
2. Pin this wing shape on to the second 6 in. piece and trim this to the same shape.
3. Finish off with sandpaper while the two pieces are still pinned together.
4. Now you have two wing panels of the same shape. Turn one over so that you have one right-hand and one left-hand wing panel laid on the table.
5. Mark two pencil lines on the top of each panel as shown—one line ½ in. (12.5 mm) from the front edge of the wing, and the other 1½ in. (37.5 mm) from the back edge of the wing.
6. Now with a knife or a small plane, cut 'flats' on the top of each wing panel as shown in the next diagram, so that the wing panels are roughly shaped like a proper wing section.
7. Wrap a piece of medium sandpaper around a solid block of wood and round off the flats. Carry on sanding until you have shaped the top of each panel into a smooth curve with a rounded front and a fairly thin back edge. Then use fine sandpaper to sand over the whole panel, top and bottom, to get it really smooth.
8. Using medium sandpaper wrapped round a block of wood, hold one panel over the edge of the table and sand off the end at an angle. Do the same with the other panel.
9. Take two short lengths of scrap balsa strip, mark off 1¼ in. (31.5 mm) on each and stick a pin through. Use these strips to hold up the tips of each wing panel with the centres brought together as shown in the final diagram. If they do not fit together neatly, trim the ends with sandpaper, or a knife, until they do.
10. The two wing panels are then cemented together. To get a really strong joint, coat the end of each panel with cement and let it dry. Then add another coat of cement and bring the two panels together, with the tips raised 1¼ in. (31.5 mm) by the strips and pins. Then run a skin of balsa cement over the centre to make the joint even stronger.
11. Leave for at least an hour for the cement to set properly.

Cutting the other parts

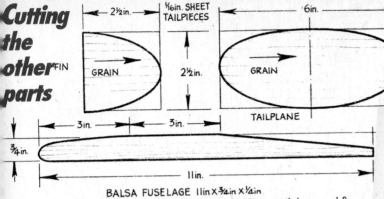

FIN

1/16in. SHEET TAILPIECES

2½in.

2½in.

GRAIN

6in.

GRAIN

MARK OUTLINE SHAPE

TAILPLANE

¾in.

3in.

3in.

11in.

BALSA FUSELAGE 11in X ¾in X ¼in

Now you can make the other parts required—the fuselage, tailplane and fin.
1. For the fuselage use a strip of hard ¾ in. x ¼ in. (19 x 6.5 mm) balsa. Cut off a 11 in. (280 mm) length and shape it.
2. The tailplane and fin are both rectangles cut from 1/16 in. (1.5 mm) sheet balsa. They can be shaped in whatever way you think looks suitable.

I HOUR LATER.

I DOOT THAT'S NO' RICHT!

WAIT A MINUTE, THOUGH—I'M BEIN' DAFT! I'M USIN' THIS PLAN THE WRONG WAY!

Assembling the model

1. The tailplane is cemented under the back end of the fuselage and the fin to one side of the fuselage, resting on top of the tail. This is safer than cementing the fin to the top of the fuselage. Hold the fin and tailplane in position with pins until set.
2. The wing joint should have set hard by now. Carefully sandpaper a 'flat' along the bottom of the wing joint so that it will sit on top of the fuselage.
3. Mark the position where the wing will be fixed—back from the front of the fuselage—and then cement in place. Hold with pins and, by looking along the model, check that the wing lines up 'square' with the tailplane.
4. Finally build up a really thick 'fillet' of cement between the bottom of the wing and the side of the fuselage on each side to get a really strong joint.

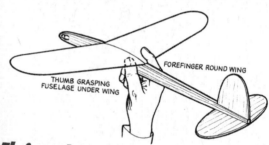

FOREFINGER ROUND WING

THUMB GRASPING FUSELAGE UNDER WING

Flying the model

1. You will need to add weight added to the nose to balance it for flying. Use Plasticine, wrapped around the front of the fuselage, adjusting the amount of weight until the model glides on as flat a path as possible.
2. If it does not glide straight, gently bend the rear edge of the tail fin to one side, and if this does not work, sight along the model to see if the fin or tailplane is out of line. Cut off and cement back on properly if this is the trouble.
3. Having trimmed your model, hold, with your forefinger resting against the edge of the right wing, alongside the fuselage. Now throw the model upwards, and watch what happens. Quite likely it will loop. Now twist the fin slightly to the right and try again. With practice, and by adjusting the amount of twist on the fin you should eventually be able to get a 'straight up' launch with the model turning immediately into a gentle, circling glide.

I had anither idea. Next morning I went tae the park. "Did ye build yer flier, Wullie?" asked Fat Bob, while Specks asked if I used the plan. "Oh, aye! I used the plan a'richt."

LOOK! THERE IT IS!

HE'S MADE A KITE WI' IT!

PLAN

HO! HO! I KENT I'D MAK' A BETTER FLIER THAN YOU, SPECKY!

GRR

HA! HA! YOURS IS DOON, SPECKY. AN' WULLIE'S IS STILL FLYIN'!

FLIERS, EH? ACH! I'M OWER FLY FOR HIM!

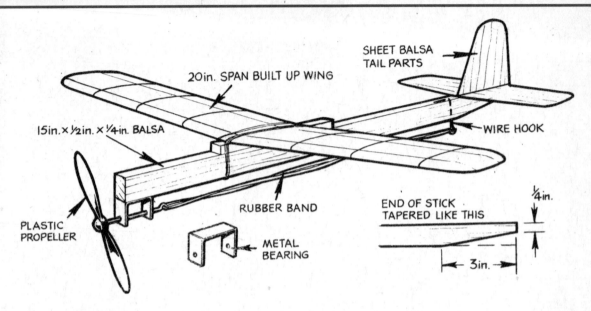

20in. SPAN BUILT UP WING

SHEET BALSA TAIL PARTS

15in. x ½in. x ¼-in. BALSA

WIRE HOOK

PLASTIC PROPELLER

RUBBER BAND

METAL BEARING

END OF STICK TAPERED LIKE THIS

¼in.

3in.

A rubber-band powered aeroplane

The fuselage is a 15 in. (380 mm) length of hard ½ in. x ¼ in. (12.5 x 6.5 mm) balsa strip or a simple stick (hence the name stick model), with a metal propeller shaft bearing bound to the front end. The rubber motor is fixed to the bottom of the stick. Tailplane and fin are cut from light 1/16 in. (1.5 mm) sheet balsa, cemented to the tail end. The built-up wing is cemented to a length of ¼ in. (6.5 mm) square balsa, attached to the stick with a rubber band. This allows the wing to be moved backwards or forwards to trim the model. A built-up wing is lighter than a solid wing. It is made up of balsa spars and ribs covered in tissue paper.

The propeller is a 5 in., 6 in. or 7 in. (130 mm, 150 mm, 180 mm) diameter plastic type, which you can buy from a model shop. The size of rubber motor needed will depend on the propeller used. Start with a single loop of ¼ in. (6.5 mm) rubber strip. If this is not enough, use twice the length of

rubber tied into a single loop and then doubled back on itself to make four strands.

Stick models are quite easy to build, and fun to fly, and you can learn a lot about rubber-powered flight from them. Try your hand at designing and building bigger stick models after studying these hints:

1. A solid stick will be too heavy for a large model. Build a hollow stick from sheet balsa sides, joined with two pieces of strip balsa at the top and bottom.
2. You can also save weight—and improve performance—by using a built-up tailplane and fin on larger models.
3. The size of the tailplane should be about one-third of the wing. The size of the fin should be about one third of the tail-plane.
4. The larger the propeller, the better the performance should be. For the best results the propeller diameter should be at least one-third of the wing span.

18

I wonder if I could mak' a rubber-band powered cartie?

Makin' model aeroplanes

Ma best model aeroplanes.
Spitfire, Mosquito,
Hurricane,
Messerschmitt Me 109,
Concorde, Lancaster,
Sunderland Flying Boat,
Comet Racer,
Tiger Moth,
Messerschmitt Me 262,
Bristol Blenheim Mk IV

JINGS!

Modelling Memories

Any boy reminiscing about his childhood is almost bound to mention the making of Airfix models. Making the first model is that great rite of passage that shows Mum and Dad that you can follow instructions and create something recognisable (well, usually) out of a disparate collection of plastic pieces.

Once hooked, so the collection of models grows, ambition sometimes exceeding actual skill, while completed models, once enjoyed began to gather dust and childish enthusiasm moves on to other interests. The experience is never forgotten and fatherhood once again brings back that enthusiasm for these collection of plastic pieces.

We owe our enthusiasm and nostalgia to a Hungarian refugee called Nicholas Kove, who founded Airfix in 1939 to make inflated rubber toys. Airfix was the name because air was fixed into these products and because the name would appear near the start of business directories.

After World War II Airfix started to make plastic combs, so it was quite a change of direction when it made a model plastic Ferguson tractor in 1949 as a promotional item for the tractor company.

The first recognisable kit, introduced in 1952, was a model of the Golden Hind, the boat in which Sir Francis Drake sailed around the world. It was followed in the next year by a model of the Supermarine Spitfire, still one of the most popular models.

Since then hundreds of models have been created, giving delight and sticky fingers to generations of modellers.

e heard that Maggie Broon daes a
t o' modellin', but surely girls dinnae like
eroplanes an' stuff like that?

Improve Your Model Making

All plastic kits are made from polystyrene, which can only be stuck together with polystyrene cement, usually called 'plastic cement'. It is no good trying to stick a plastic model together with balsa cement, for example. It just will not work.

You have probably built several plastic kits already, but has every one worked out as well as you would have liked? There may be gaps at some of the joints, surplus cement smeared on the surfaces and spoiling the appearance, and other small faults that show up. The following tips should help improve your model making.

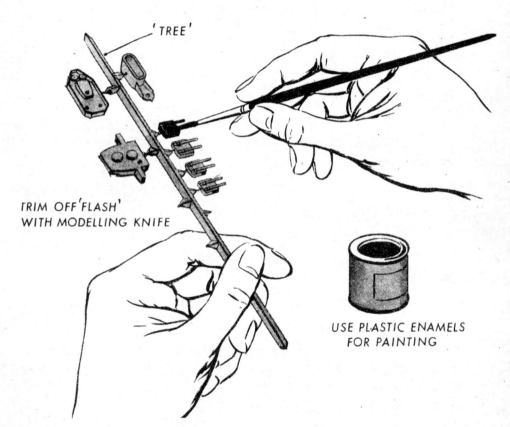

'TREE'

TRIM OFF 'FLASH' WITH MODELLING KNIFE

USE PLASTIC ENAMELS FOR PAINTING

Care with model kits

Firstly, the small parts of the plastic 'tree' are much better cut off with a modelling knife than broken off. But before you do this, examine the part carefully and see if it has a thin web of plastic sticking to it. This is called 'flash' and is surplus plastic. This should be cut off carefully with a modelling knife while the part is still on the tree and easy to hold.

Before you cut the part see if it needs painting. If so, it is best to paint it while it is still on the tree. As a general rule, the more parts that can be painted before cementing together the better.

10

Learn to cement joints

For the really important job of joining the parts of your model together, first check that the parts fit properly. If parts do not fit with a hairline joint between them, the edges may need trimming. You can do this by scraping the plastic with a modelling knife, or use a small flat file to trim the edges.

The way to apply cement is not by squeezing it straight from the tube on to the joint. Instead, squeeze a little cement into a small tin lid. The cement is quite thin but if it appears to be as thick as balsa cement it needs thinning down. This you can do by adding a little cleaning fluid and stirring. Now apply the cement to the joint with a small paintbrush. Be sure not to let any cement run over the outside edge of the joint.

The parts should then be brought together and clamped or held in position, using clothes pegs, or rubber bands, taking care not to smear the cement line. Now leave them for at least an hour for the cement to set really hard. Until the cement has set the plastic itself around the joint will be soft, and if the assembly is handled too much in this state it can be ruined.

Checking for cracks

Before adding the smaller detail parts, check over the main assembly for cracks or defects in the joint lines. These can be filled in with a special filler called body putty. This should be applied with a special tool made by sharpening the end of a small wood dowel to a chisel point. When the putty is quite dry it can be sanded down smooth to blend with the rest of the plastic, using the finest grade of wet or dry abrasive paper.

Small parts

Small parts to be assembled on the main model should be handled with tweezers. They can then be touched with the lightest dab of cement and positioned carefully. If handled

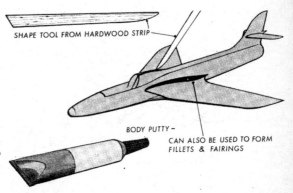

SHAPE TOOL FROM HARDWOOD STRIP

BODY PUTTY –
CAN ALSO BE USED TO FORM FILLETS & FAIRINGS

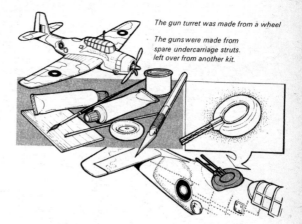

The gun turret was made from a wheel

The guns were made from spare undercarriage struts. left over from another kit.

with fingers they will be more awkward to position and there is always a chance that you will get cement on your fingers and smear it over the rest of the model.

Save the spares

Save any spare parts left over from plastic kits. Also never throw an old kit away. Some of the parts may be very useful for modifying or improving a later kit model. Thin wires, for example, can be made by touching a left-over plastic tree with the end of a piece of heated wire and then drawing off a thread of plastic. Some idea of what can be done in modifying plastic kit models is shown. This should give you several other ideas to work on. Then, instead of having the same model as thousands of others who have bought the same kit, you have a completely individual one.

An' I made a better flier than yon mad inventors. Wha's the clever ane aboot here!

Inventors Patent Odd Designs

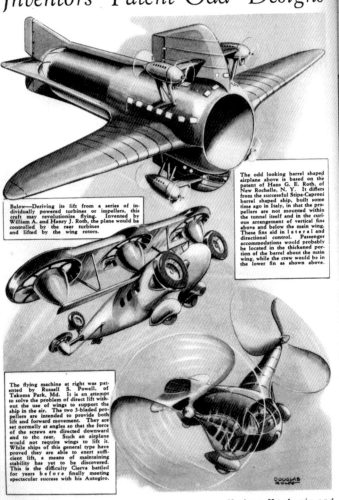

The odd looking barrel shaped airplane above is based on the patent of Hans G. E. Roth, of New Rochelle, N. Y. It differs from the successful Stipa-Caproni barrel shaped ship, built some time ago in Italy, in that the propellers are not mounted within the tunnel itself and in the curious arrangement of vertical fins above and below the main wing. These fins aid in lateral and directional control. Passenger accommodations would probably be located in the thickened portion of the barrel about the main wing, while the crew would be in the lower fin as shown above.

Below—Deriving its lift from a series of individually powered turbines or impellers, this craft may revolutionize flying. Invented by William A. and Henry J. Roth, the plane would be controlled by the rear turbines and lifted by the wing rotors.

The flying machine at right was patented by Russell S. Powell, of Takoma Park, Md. It is an attempt to solve the problem of direct lift without the use of wings to support the ship in the air. The two 3-bladed propellers are intended to provide both lift and forward movement. They are set normally at angles so that the force of the screws are directed downward and to the rear. Such an airplane would not require wings to lift it. While ships of this general type have proved they are able to exert sufficient lift, a means of maintaining stability has yet to be discovered. This is the difficulty Cierva battled for years before finally meeting spectacular success with his Autogiro.

82

FOR SAFER AIRPLAN

by DOUGLAS ROLFE

Unusual ships, straying away from accepted designs, are being tried in an effort to increase safety and simplify air travel. Some of the ideas are shown here.

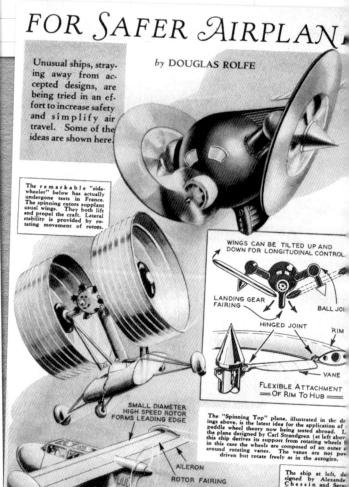

The remarkable "side-wheeler" below has actually undergone tests in France. The spinning rotors supplant usual wings. They both lift and propel the craft. Lateral stability is provided by rotating movement of rotors.

WINGS CAN BE TILTED UP AND DOWN FOR LONGITUDINAL CONTROL

LANDING GEAR FAIRING

BALL JOI

HINGED JOINT

RIM

VANE

FLEXIBLE ATTACHMENT OF RIM TO HUB

SMALL DIAMETER HIGH SPEED ROTOR FORMS LEADING EDGE

AILERON

ROTOR FAIRING

The "Spinning Top" plane, illustrated in the dr ings above, is the latest idea for the application of paddle wheel theory now being tested abroad. the plane designed by Carl Strandgren (at left abov this ship derives its support from rotating wheels in this case the wheels are composed of an outer around rotating vanes. The vanes are not pow driven but rotate freely as in the autogiro.

The ship at left, de signed by Alexande Chessin and Serg Trey, is intended to improve safe flying. A 12-inch hollow cylin der, 23 feet long form the leading edge of the wing. Built on the Flettner rotor principle, it rotates 7,000 r. p. m. A constant stream of air is directed onto the cylinder by tiny jets to insure continuous lift.

Inventions, May, 1935

Balloons

Ye can hae lots o' fun an' games wi'
balloons, ye ken that! But did ye
ken that a balloon an' a jet engine
hae something in common?

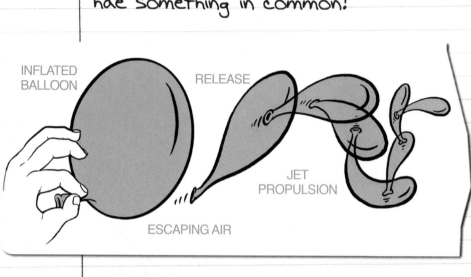

INFLATED
BALLOON

RELEASE

JET
PROPULSION

ESCAPING AIR

SCHOOL PROJECT - Jet balloon

I ken that ye've done this many times. Blaw up a
balloon, an', instead o' tyin' a knot tae keep the air in,
jist let it go. It will zip aboot the room, makin' a rude
noise as it goes. It's braw!

I couldna believe it when ma teacher let a balloon loose
in oor classroom. We should dae that, no' him! He said it
shows how a jet engine works. The air rushes oot o'
the balloon tae mak' it go forward.

I must try fixin' a balloon tae ma model flier an' see how
it goes.

Kites

I'm a great ane for kites, flyin' high an'
swoppin' doon fae the sky. Ye can mak'
yer ain or there are lots ye can buy.

HANDY PROJECTS

Making a Kite - *A tethered kite*

Make a kite from three 10 in. (250 mm) lengths of ¼ x ¼ in. (6.5 x 6.5 mm) strip
balsa for the frame pieces, pinned together through the centre and opened out. Add
an outline of thread and cover the kite with paper, light cotton or nylon fabric. Add
bridle lines and a tail, as shown.

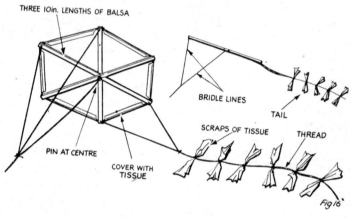

THREE 10in. LENGTHS OF BALSA

PIN AT CENTRE

COVER WITH TISSUE

BRIDLE LINES

TAIL

SCRAPS OF TISSUE

THREAD

Fig 16

This model will fly quite well. It develops lift just like a fixed wing, being held by the
bridle at an angle to the wind. The tail simply keeps it heading into the wind.

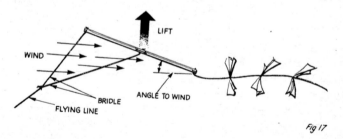

LIFT

WIND

BRIDLE

FLYING LINE

ANGLE TO WIND

Fig 17

The fact that the wing is tethered by the bridle prevents the wing slipping sideways.
If the bridle lines are not the right length, and equal on each side, the kite will not
be stable.

WULLIE'S WISDOMS

Every cloud has
a silver lining.

A box kite

A box kite is an even better flyer—more stable and developing even more lift for its size. You can make a box kite, again using balsa strip for the sticks, and paper, light cotton or nylon fabric for the panels. The box kite is stable enough to be flown on a single line—that is, you do not require a bridle—provided you attach the line in the right place.

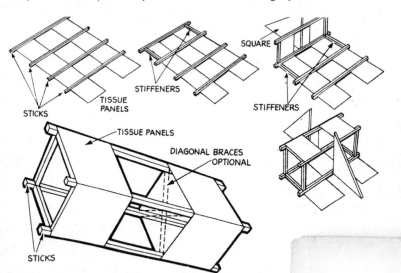

Fat Bob got a pressie o' a Chinese kite — it wis ower bonnie tae fly, an' we couldnae mak' sense o' the instructions.

风筝

DESCRIPTION

Kite is a traditional Chinese folk art with a long history. The Tientsin Kites are quite distinctive in their process pattern design, colour and style. They are characteristic of fine ribs and convenience of knocking down. By inheriting the special features of Chinese paintings, wood engravings and Tientsin Yang Liu Ching annual painting, the designs on Kites are presenting clear-cut line, bright and fresh colour and vivid appearance.

Kite-flying is not only a form of helpful recreation but also a sporting activity for physical exercises as well as increasing sight ability and distinguishing wind direction and force. So far as how to fly kites, it is suitable to find a spacious square under about gentle breeze.

Before flying kites you should firstly fasten every part of the assemblage. Secondly you have to adjust the top cord to accord with wind force. It is necessary to shorten upper of the top cord, if the wind is strong, or shorten the lower if weak. If the kites fly unsteadily with head downward, then shorten upper string of top cord. If the Kites do not fly upward but drop slowly, just shorten the upper string. With such an adjustment, the Kites can steadily fly up to an optimum height.

Parachutes

Wha'd hae thocht that auld Leonardo da Vinci invented the parachute afore we could even fly.

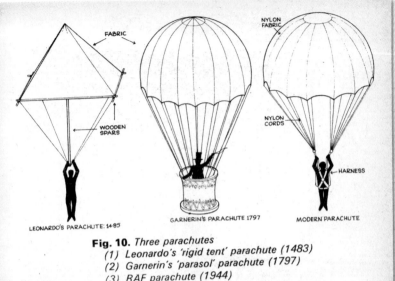

Fig. 10. Three parachutes
(1) Leonardo's 'rigid tent' parachute (1483)
(2) Garnerin's 'parasol' parachute (1797)
(3) RAF parachute (1944)

But then mebbe he kent aboot the dandelion. If ye pick a dandelion seed head on a windy day an' blaw, each seed is carried away by a wee parachute – but dinna try this near gairdens. Nae gairdener likes dandelions.

AUCHENSHOOGLE POLICE STATION
DATE ..... *Wednesday 18th*
POLICE CONSTABLE ..... *Murdoch*

Wednesday – Headquarters want me to show a new colleague the ropes. It's a woman police officer from the big city, and she's being parachuted in to learn about small town policing!
I'll be like a father figure I suppose, with all my experience. I need to figure out a way of getting a bit of respect from Wullie and his pals.

Had tae call an urgent gang meetin' at ma shed.
Told the lads that there's another polis bein' parachuted in.
Eck said mebbe we cause so much trouble, they need twa polis tae cope.
Bob thinks mebbe he's retirin'? We cannae let that happen!
Mebbe he wis jokin'?
What if it's a champion polis that can run and no' get oot o' puff and catch up wi' us?

Make a parachute

Have ye ever made a parachute oot o' an auld hankie?

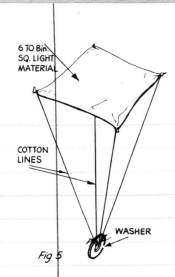

6 TO 8in. SQ. LIGHT MATERIAL

COTTON LINES

WASHER

Fig 5

Tie some cotton thread tae each corner. Then tie the free ends thegither, makin' sure each piece o' cotton is the same length. Then tie on a weight – ask yer Pa for a washer.

LIFT UP AT CORNERS, THEN FOLD INTO BALL

Pick yer parchute up by the middle o' the hankie. Now drap it an' watch it float doon. Try using an upstairs windie. P.C. Murdoch wis richt puzzled when a parachute drapped at his feet! Try this, haud the parachute upside doon an' lower it ontae a table. Drap the weight intae the centre, an' fold the parachute up intae a ba'. Now throw this ba' up in the air an' the watch it glide back tae earth.

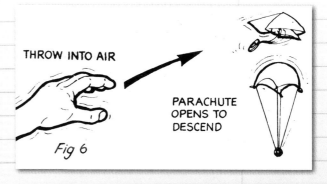

THROW INTO AIR

PARACHUTE OPENS TO DESCEND

Fig 6

BUT – NEXT DAY.

JINGS! HE WISNA JOKIN'! THERE'S TWA O' THEM, RIGHT ENOUGH!

A WOMAN BOBBY?

WULLIE!

HELP! WHAT HAVE I DONE NOW?

COME BACK HERE!

NO FEAR!

AT WULLIE'S SHED.

AHA! THERE YE ARE! I THOCHT YE'D COME HERE!

B-BUT WHIT HAVE I DONE?

DONE? NOTHING! BUT I HAD TAE GET AWA' FROM THAT WOMAN! SHE'S HAD ME POLISHIN' MY BUTTONS TWICE ALREADY – AN' SHE HASNA LET ME GET A QUIET SMOKE A' DAY!

Wullie's Fund-Raisin' Scheme

Ye can use yer skills at makin' things tae mak' useful machines. I made a braw machine tae wash windies.

When I turn the handle the mop goes roond an' when I pump the bellows the water squirts oot o' the hose.

I tried tae clean Mrs McAteer's windies, but ended up cleaning P.C Murdoch . . .

Ma said I could clean the windies at hame, but the machine broke an' smashed a windie.

I had an idea: tak' the glass oot o' the windie, then Pa will think it is really clean.

An' I fooled him! He wis goin' tae gie me a shillin'.

Jist remember, a fool an' his money are easily parted.

Wooden toys

There are a' kinds o' toys ye can mak' fae wood. Ma favourite is the cotton-reel tank.

WOODEN TOYS TO MAKE

Making a cotton-reel tank: A very simple rubber-powered model is shown in the diagram. For this you need:
- a cotton reel;
- a short rubber band;
- a toothpick (or a piece of thin wood about 4 in. (100 mm) long);
- a slice about ¼ in. (6.5 mm) thick cut off the end of a candle;
- a matchstick;
- a pin (bent into a U-shape, as shown).

Make a hole through the centre of the slice of candle and assemble the model as shown. The matchstick is passed through the other end of the rubber band and held to the side of the cotton reel with the bent pin.

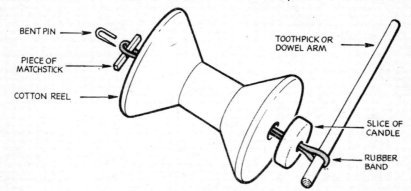

Wind up the model by turning the arm round and round about twenty times, then place it on a flat surface. It should crawl forward at a slow speed as the rubber band unwinds. You will find that this little tank has enough power to climb over small obstacles placed in its way.

Here are some other things you can try with this type of model:
- Try using different sizes of rubber bands and cotton reel.
- Build two or three different models and have speed and climbing trials. To make a better 'climber', cut notches in the edges of the cotton reel; or stretch a short rubber band around each edge.

An' there are hunners o' ither things ye can mak' wi' wood. It's no' difficult, an' mebbe ye can sell them tae yer family an' their friends. That's ma tip for the day. If ye canna be doin' wi' makin' toys, try ma simple suggestions usin' pine cones.

Make a locomotive

Various designs you can make are shown in the diagram. The locomotive (A) needs a base cut from ½ in. (12.5 mm) thick sheet for a toy up to about 6 in. (150 mm) long; and thicker sheet for a larger toy. The rest of the shape is then built up from block pieces, and suitable sizes of dowel cut to length. Glue and nail these in place through the bottom of the base—except for the funnel, of course, which is nailed directly on top of the boiler.

Make a truck

Trucks are just as simple to make. The open truck (B) has a thick base piece again, with the ends and sides made from the thinner sheet; A covered wagon can be a solid block of/wood (C), with the axles driven straight into the sides Couplings are made from brass screw-eyes, one eye being opened up into a hook-shape to fit into the eye of the coupling in front of it.

WULLIE'S WISDOMS

Like faither, like son.

101 THINGS TAE DAE WI' A BUCKET

No. 99 CHRISTMAS STOCKING

I asked Santa Claus tae bring me a machine buildin' set so that Pa could play wi' it an' gie me some peace tae play wi' ma ain toys.

Making lorries

The other designs shown are just as simple to make. The lorry (D) is straightforward, provided you use a thick enough piece for the base. The articulated lorry (E) is a little more tricky for you need an additional beam under the back of the base of the tractor part to carry the smaller wheels. It will be best to drill holes in the end of this beam to take the nail axles to make sure that these do not split the wood. The short length of dowel is simply glued into a hole drilled down from the top. A slightly larger hole drilled in the bottom of solid truck body provides a means of fitting the two together.

The trickiest job with this toy is getting all the wheels fitted properly. Fit only one pair of the truck wheels first. Then couple the truck to the tractor and find out exactly the right height for the 'axles' for the other pair of wheels.

Toys like this can be made up from simple 'block' shapes. There is no reason why these shapes should not be rounded off, or cut to different shapes to make them more realistic. Most of this shaping can be done before the blocks are finally fitted in position.

Wooden toys like this should always be assembled with glued joints. Parts can be nailed together as well, mainly to hold them in place while the glue is setting. If you are making them for small children, use wood screws instead of nails to hold the parts together. This will give an almost unbreakable assembly

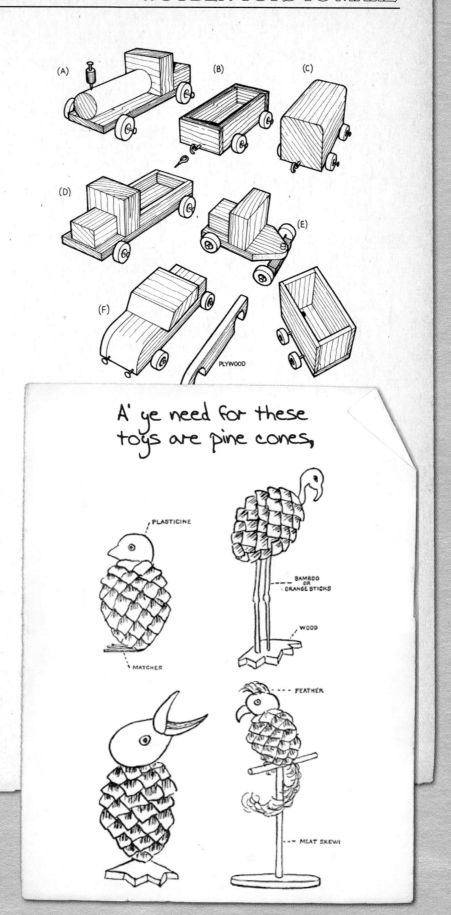

A' ye need for these toys are pine cones,

Making a fort
An' finally, if ye hae a wee brother, ask yer Pa tae mak' a fort for him tae use wi' his model sojers. Any dad should find this easy – an' tell him I said so!

Goodies

WOODWORKING WEEKLY

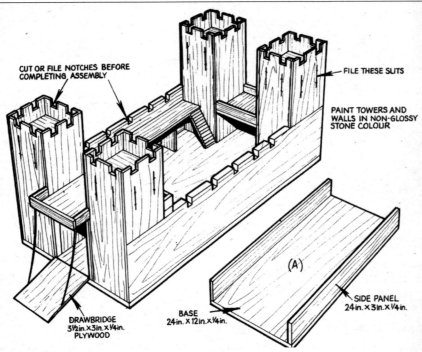

CUT OR FILE NOTCHES BEFORE COMPLETING ASSEMBLY

FILE THESE SLITS

PAINT TOWERS AND WALLS IN NON-GLOSSY STONE COLOUR

(A)

DRAWBRIDGE
3½ in. × 3 in. × ¼ in.
PLYWOOD

BASE
24 in. × 12 in. × ¼ in.

SIDE PANEL
24 in. × 3 in. × ¼ in.

Making a fort

This is a design for a 24 in. x 12 in. (600 x 300 mm) model fort, made mainly from ¼ in. (6.5 mm) and ⅛ in. (3 mm) obechi sheet. The base can be cut from ⅜ in. (9.5 mm) plywood, or you can use hardboard fitted with a framework of ½ in. (12.5 mm) square softwood strip to strengthen it.

Making the framework

Start by gluing the sides to the base, taking care to get them upright. The pieces for the four towers are then cut from ⅛ in. sheet obechi, marking them out to the dimensions shown. All four towers are identified and are glued in position at each corner of the base. The notches in the tops of the tower pieces should all be cut before the towers are assembled.

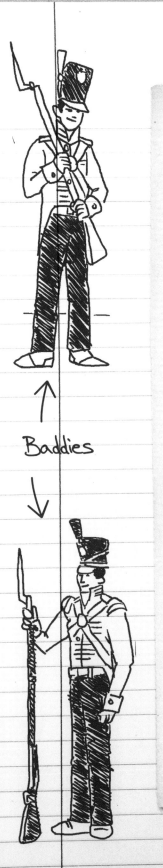

Baddies

Fit the galleries and drawbridge

The rest of the parts are fairly straightforward to cut and fit. Tackle them in this order:

1. Cut and fit the pieces to complete the end wall between two of the towers. Glue all parts in place.

2. Cut the side gallery pieces from ⅛ in. sheet and support on uprights, glued in place.

3. Cut the parts for the drawbridge and gallery and glue in place. For the extension piece which juts out over the front, you will have to glue two 3 in. (75 mm) wide pieces of obechi sheets together, or you can cut this from ⅛ in. ply or hardboard.

4. Make and fit the drawbridge. This can be fastened to the bay with a proper hinge and small screws, or you can use tape strips glued in place to form a hinge. The hinge wants to be 'free' enough for the drawbridge to drop down under its own weight. Take the two drawbridge strings up through holes in the gallery so that you can pull on these from the inside of the fort to raise the drawbridge. Join the two strings with a knot and drive in a small nail at some convenient point to loop the strings over to hold the drawbridge up.

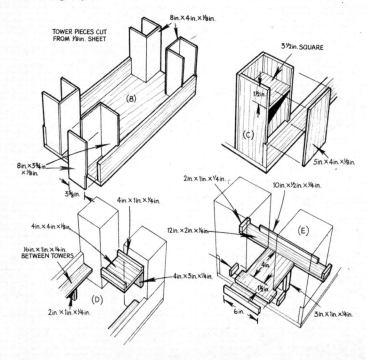

Finally paint the whole model in a realistic colour. Emulsion paint will be best as this will dry without any gloss and you can get it in 'stone' colours.

9

87

Makin' a robot

This wis ae o' ma best creations!

Fat Bob an' Soapy Soutar tricked me oot o' seeing a robot film, so I decided tae mak' a robot tae trick them.

I worked hard in ma shed wi' lots o' boxes, an' sticky tape an' silver paint. When I hae finished, I left the shed.

Soon they came in an' saw the robot. Fat Bob turned its switch on an' got a great surprise! He never thocht it would work.

It picked an apple aff a stall an' it even gied 'em both a punch.

But mebbe ye've guessed it wis really me. It wis great bein' a robot

Wullie's Fund-Raisin' Scheme

Anither way tae raise cash is tae collect things that some dinnae want an' then sell them tae ither fowk that want them. That's the best business tip I can gie ye — now follow my example an' mak' yer fortune.

It a' started when Ma gave me an auld record player tae tak' tae the dump...

But I didna reach the dump. I sellt the horn tae a salesman who wis losing his voice,

an' I got a shillin' for the turntable,

an' I got twa bob for the handle,

an' I sellt the spring, an' ither bits an' a'. So much for it bein' rubbish!

PART 5 - Doin' things ootdoors.

Campin' - There's nothin' better than campin' in the summer, but ye need tae learn a few basics.

Find a guid spot tae camp, wi' nae noise or ferm animals, so ye can get yer rest.

HEATING UP SOUP WHEN OUT CAMPING

Dinna tak' ower much wi' you.

Go wi' friends so they can dae a lot o' the work

FAVOORITE SPOTS
FOR CAMPIN'
BERKY BRAES
BERRY HILL
STOORIE HILL
NEAR THE RIVER

Tak' some food.

An' if I'm campin' nearby, I tak' MA BUCKET an' the cartie.

THINGS TAE TAK' CAMPIN'

BUCKET
SLEEPING BAG
TENT (WELL, I DID ONCE FORGET)
CANDLE
TORCH
ANTI-MIDGIE STUFF
FOOD
MATCHES
PLATE AN' MUG
KNIFE, FORK AN' SPOON
TIN OPENER
MAP
WATERPROOF

101 THINGS TAE DAE WI' A BUCKET

No. 41

STOPS FOOD GETTIN SQUASHED WHEN YOU'RE CAMPING (HANDS OFF FAT BOAB!)

101 THINGS TAE DAE WI' A BUCKET

No. 48 FOR SITTIN' ON - SIMPLE!

Happy campin'!

If ye need some help I've stuck in some bits fae a magazine.

101 THINGS TAE DAE WI' A BUCKET

No. 20

CATCHING FISH. (GOT TO BE QUICK THOUGH!)

FIND A CAMP SITE

Near every city and town is rough country ideal for camping. Make a reconnaissance there on foot or bike. If you live in a village it is obvious: you want the roughest country nearest to—yet outside—your local community.

Instead of fields, riversides and orchards, look for patches of grass among rock outcrops, gorse bushes, bracken knolls, pine trees, stunted hawthorns, glinting streams, old walls and heathery hills. And with maybe a night-view of your town lit up below like an airport from the sky. A sheltered camp site is vital. Aim to have the tent's entrance away from the wind.

Out-of-the-way-sites are better than those on parks in the town where you see too many people. Here, no one will cross your path. And as the tent will be hidden in the jumbled terrain, you only need ask permission if there is a farm nearby. (It there is, you must ask.) Here are some ideal sites.

WHAT TO LOOK FOR

- High, dry, level turf shielded by a wall, rock outcrop or wood (so the bivvy can be in the lee, entrance away from the wind).
- A spot which will catch sun early in the morning.
- Pick ground where water cannot stay in pools
- A stream with fish in it above any houses (it will probably be fresh).
- Plenty of wood (but keep away from forests because of FIRE RISK).

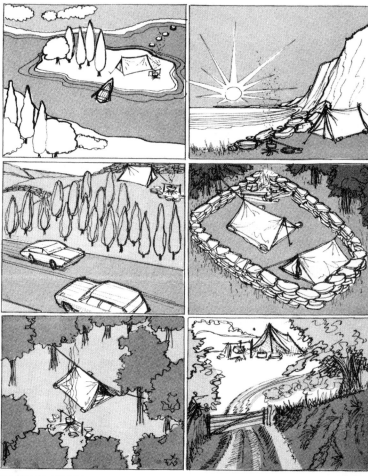

WHAT TO AVOID

- Trees right above (to cut out sun, let in lightning).
- Long grass (to attract bugs).
- Stagnant back-waters under water lilies or willows (which breed mosquitoes, mists, chills).

- Low-level, clay or boggy ground (ditto) and sandbanks (also ditto).
- Horses/cows/pigs (which attack tents).
- Busy roads or rushing noisy water.

Ma guide tae guid campin'

Pa came campin' wi me once. He learnt a lot.

1. Select the best site. Dinna listen tae onyone wha's feart. Pa didna want tae camp in the forest because it wis dark.

2. Keep an eye on the tent. We had a visitor.

3. Dinna be feart o' noises in the nicht. That's part o' campin'. It could be an owl, a tree branch creakin', sheep movin' aboot, wind in the bracken, a rabbit skitterin' past. Noises seem loudest the first nicht.

4. Dinna abandon camp in the nicht, unless it's worth it!

Ye dinna hae tae camp wi' a tent.
Here's how tae bivouac (Pa'll no want tae dae that).

How to make a bivouac

You need: a sheet of heavy-grade horticultural polythene anywhere from 8 ft. x 8 ft. to 10 ft. x 10 ft.; plenty of hairy string and four tent pegs. Everything else is part of the landscape—apart from the groundsheet which can be a strip of thinner polythene big enough to lie on.

You can make one of these three kinds of bivouac in ANY rough country. Which type you use depends on the terrain: whether you are among woods, rocks, trees or just a lot of barren ground.

The A-type can be made between two piles of stones, rucksack frames, thick branches, ice axes or even bicycles as tent posts—as long as there are heavy stones to provide tension.

It's best to tie the string in advance to the bivvy sheet Then, no matter where you camp, you can put up your shelter in minutes. Use marbles or smooth pebbles to help tie the string to the plastic as shown.

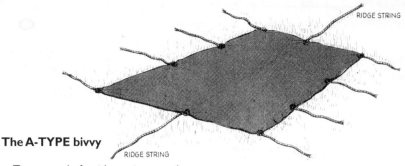

RIDGE STRING

RIDGE STRING

The A-TYPE bivvy

Tie one end of a ridge string round a tree, fence post or boulder (about 3 ft. from the grass). Wind the opposite ridge string twice round anything over 3 ft. high, preferably a thick stick. Pull the far ridge string taut and tie the end round a heavy rock. Shift the rock back until the bivvy sheet looks as if it is hanging from its ridge.

The four tent pegs are used to pin the sheet corners to the ground, so roughing out the shape of the A-type shelter. Do not stick them through the plastic: wrap the strings each round a peg several times instead.

Remove the pegs, one by one, and substitute them for four big stones tied to each corner with half hitches.

Now tie stones to the two centre strings on each side. And pull all the stones (nine in all) outwards. Pad between the stones and polythene with grass or moss to stop chafing.

Note: when windy the ridge can be one long piece of string—like a clothesline. The bivvy is hung over it. There is less risk of the plastic ripping.

The Lean-To

Bivvies can be built against a wall, big rock or hedge. The wall is most common. Jam strong twigs between the stones about 5 ft. up. Knot the bivvy's top edge strings to these. Or thread the string through chinks and tie. Never use wall top-stones as string anchors: they drop on you. But you can pass string over the wall and hang rocks down the other side. Anchor the bottom edge with four rocks as for the A-type bivvy. Pull the sheet tight.

The Wigwam

As shown; build against a tree. Best for woods on hot days. This one has most headroom but can be draughty.

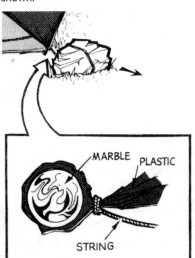

MARBLE   PLASTIC

STRING

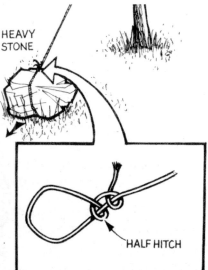

HEAVY STONE

HALF HITCH

When you fold the bivvy sheet up, just tuck the bits of string inside and out of the way. Do not untie them.

Now try making the three kinds of bivouac on your lawn or in the park. Take your time. Make sure each one you make is really taut and solid before taking it down and going on to the next.

THE 'A' TYPE BIVVY   THE LEAN-TO

THE WIGWAM

The camp fire

The camp fire really makes campin' fun. But ye need tae know how tae mak' a fire.

Collect firewood (sma' bits for startin' the fire an' larger bits for heat).

P.C. Murdoch reminded me tae say that ye should only gather up fallen wood (wood that is deid an' on the ground). Never cut wood fae growin' trees or bushes.

Build the camp fire an' light it wi' matches. If ye've forgotten the matches, ye can use the sparks fae tacketty boots!

Ye can cook yer food on the fire an' then sit roond it tae sing campfire songs. The fire helps tae keep the midges an' flies away an' a'.

95

Ye need tae be careful wi' fires, an' this guide micht help.

COLLECTING FIREWOOD

Gather loads of it. You cannot collect enough. Brittle, dry wood is best. The driest branches have no bark and never feel cold. COLD wood is damp and heavy: useless for fires unless you can get flames going to thaw out this wood first. You can find dry, tindery wood—even after rain— by looking under dense shrubbery, or snapping dead branches off trees. Never start a fire with branches still bearing leaves. Thick dead limbs of old oaks are good; so is some wet-looking wood which you can cut away with a knife to reveal a dry core. Try everything that looks possible. But gather a big wood pile first.

LIGHTING A CAMP FIRE

First, you must scrape the ground in a 6 ft. circle round the hearth so flying sparks are not dangerous. Then set up a mini-pyramid of bits of paper, wood shavings, dry wood powder, brittle leaves, birch bark, little twigs and fluff from your pocket linings. Lay bits of wood over these and strike a match. The kindling flares up, briefly licks the heavier wood and . . . goes out. Try again. This time the top wood collapses and squashes the kindling flat. So lay down and puff at the fire, mouth to the twigs. Still no good. With a black face and filthy hands you begin to swear. . . yet you were nearly there. The kindling pyramid was good. But you laid wood that was too heavy on top. And it wasn't softwood: hazel, pine, spruce or fir. These are great in twigs on top of the kindling. And you can pile hardwood bits on these: oak, beech, birch, poplar. Use the paper-thin outer layer of birchbark as a superb fire booster. Thread it in through chinks in the twigs.

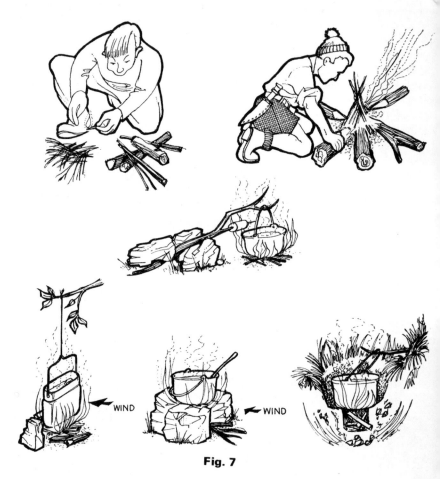

WIND

WIND

Fig. 7

Add heavier chunks of wood to the growing fire. Circling the flames with short thick logs like the spokes of a wheel helps: keep nudging them into the fire. Cover the flames with a pile of ashes to keep coals hot overnight. Next morning clear away the ashes and make the coals glow by blowing on them.

Cookin'
Remember tae tak' food wi' ye an'
somebody that can cook! If ye tak'
food in cans, ye must open the tins
afore ye heat them. That's ma best tip.

Ane o' Pa's mates gave me these
suggestions for campfire food. No' sure
aboot an egg in an orange!

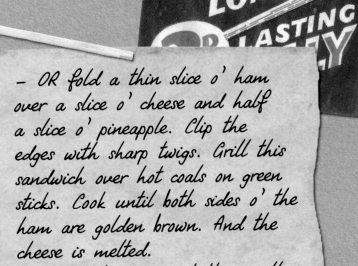

Cook what YOU like. Try some o'
these recipes too.
– Bury a big potato wrapped in
mud or aluminium foil in the
edge o' the fire.
– Thirty minutes later eat half a
carefully peeled orange and pour an
egg into the empty half o' rind.
Stick this upright in the coals too.
– Now fry bacon on a stick, or a
flat stone that is so hot any water
shoots off it.
– Then toast bread on a stick.
– After doing the egg twenty
minutes, bring out the potato,
butter it and eat it with the egg,
bacon and anything else you, cooked
too (like sausages).
– The last half o' the orange is
for pudding.

– OR cook an egg in bread on a
hot stone.

– OR fold a thin slice o' ham
over a slice o' cheese and half
a slice o' pineapple. Clip the
edges with sharp twigs. Grill this
sandwich over hot coals on green
sticks. Cook until both sides o' the
ham are golden brown. And the
cheese is melted.
– OR prick an egg at the small
end, set it up in the coals (hole
at the top) and cook for 20 min.
– OR just open tinned food you
like, heat and eat.

Next morning
– Blow the fire back to life
after cleaning the top ashes. Place
kindling on the embers and fan
into flames. Boil water for coffee/
tea, then cook bacon and eggs.
Porridge is good when soaked
overnight in salt and water.

Wullie
Please follow these instructions at the end o' your camp.

Clear everything away: EVERY speck o' salt, egg shell, charred paper, breadcrumbs, silverfoil.
• Hammer tins flat and take them home.
• Burn paper, then put the fire out with water and tread the ashes down (do not kick them).
• Put stones and earth on to the fireplace.
• Pack the bivvy sheet last after letting it dry in the sun. Or just shake the dew drops off.

Ma's recommendation

If ye hae nae bread, try cooking dampers.
Take some self-raising flour, add some salt and then mix slowly wi' enough water tae make a doughy paste.
Find some long sticks and peel aff the bark at the end.
Wrap the dough mix around this end an' place them above a glowin' fire until they are cooked.
Best eaten wi' butter and jam.

Now it's back tae Ma's cooking an' a guid nicht's rest in ma ain bed!

Anuimal tracks

If ye're oot an' aboot in the toon or country, it's guid tae ken wha leaves whit tracks. I am awfy keen tae ken the tracks o' P.C. Murdoch.

P.C. Murdoch standin'

P.C. Murdoch runnin'

Young Nature Watcher

Tracks and Trails

When a night of rain has turned the woodland paths into muddy streams, or when the first snows of winter have given these paths a light covering of snow, you will find striking evidence of the animal life around you. Most animals are secretive and you only become aware of their presence by the tracks they leave behind them. These are most easily seen in patches of mud or on frsh snow.

Here are some single footprints. You can see how much they differ from each other.

One footprint is called a track. A number of tracks together is called a trail and you can learn to read a trail. The fox, for example, has a normal trail like the one shown below.

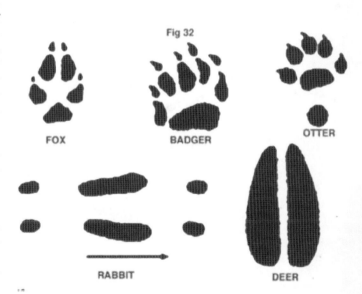

Fig 32

FOX   BADGER   OTTER

RABBIT   DEER

FOX ⟶

When a fox walks normally it place one foot directly in front of the other so that the impressions appear evenly spaced and some 10 in. (250 mm) apart. If the fox was trotting then you would see a slightly different pattern. The gap between the prints would be 14-18 in. (350-450 mm). If it were running the prints would look entirely different. The footprints would be closely packed in groups of four but each group would be spaced out with about 20 in. (500 mm) between each group.

Mountain Lion in oor toon

It wis on the radio that a Cougar has escaped fae the zoo. Miles awa' fae us - but cougars can run awfy fast. I looked it up in the incyclepedya - Jings ! it's a mountain lion. We volunteered oor services tae P.C. Murdoch tae join the search party but he just laughed and sent us awa' -"Dinna be so daft" he said. We showed him ! We cut auld bits o' lino into Lion track shapes and stuck them on our boots and went trampin' aboot in the bushes, then Fat Bob stuck a note through P.C. Murdoch's door reportin' sightin' a lion.

Never seen so many Polis in oor toon !

Young Nature Watcher

PLASTER OF PARIS

WATER

BOX WITH LID AND BASE REMOVED

COMPLETE CAST

Making a cast of tracks

Find a clear footprint in the mud. Let it dry out completely and then make a plaster cast of that track. You will need a packet of plaster of paris (obtainable from craft shops). Follow the instructions for mixing the plaster of paris very carefully.

Use the outside of a small cardboard box, with the lid removed, and place this round the footprint. Fill this with your plaster mixture and allow it to dry. When it is completely dry, carefully lift it from the ground. You should have a clear impression of the pad markings of the animal which made the track. Label the cast with the date and the details of the animal as well as full details of where you found the track.

ch Jeemy, ye're
kin' an awfy mess
o' ma book!

101

Hill walkin'

Wi' a' the hills roond and aboot, Pa likes tae go hill walkin' wi' his mates. When I ask him whit for he tells me "because they're there". Whit sort o' an answer is that! An' why does he climb Munros? I thocht they lived in the hoose doon the road.

Me hill-restin'

10   Munro Baggers Monthly

What is a Munro?

A Munro is a Scottish hill that is 3,000 ft or over in height. There are currently 283 peaks, and every so often the number changes as surveying methods become more accurate. These peaks are called Munros after Sir Hugh Thomas Munro, a Victorian landowner, born in 1856. In 1891 he was asked by the editor of the Scottish Mountaineering Club's Journal to produce a list of all Scottish hills above 3,000 ft. Within five months he published his first list, which contained 283 separate mountains. There have been various revisions over time and, with the latest revisions, the list is back to 283 Munros (though slightly different from the original list). 'Munro-bagging' (climbing all the Munros) has become a major challenge. Many try and over 4,500 people are known to have succeeded.

101 THINGS TAE DAE WI' A BUCKET

No.16

TAE COOL AFF YER FEET AFTER HIKING.

Ben Nevis

Highest hill in Scotland is Ben Nevis, 4,409 feet (1,344 metres) hig[h]

Ither high hills are:
Ben Macdui
Cairn Gorm
Aonach Mor
Ben Lawers

(there's hunners mair, o' course)

I went tae a lecture aboot Mount Everest.

But Scottish hills are tiddlers. Mount Everest is a muckle 29,029 ft. (8,848 m) high.

Next day we set aff tae climb Docken Hill, a' roped up an' wi' oor ice axes, as the man said.

An' we made it!

But a gamie stopped us on the way doon.

An' the lecturer had said bein' roped up wis for safety.

103

Surviving

I've read aboot fowk who hae survived in the wilderness. I couldna dae that – I like ma bed an' Ma's cookin' tae much. If ye do go oot into the hills ye best take a survival kit jist in case. I'll stick tae my gairden survival kit.

For when I go on a big adventure, I saved this.

↓

MA SURVIVAL KIT FOR CAMPIN' IN THE GAIRDEN

TORCH, ANTI-MIDGIE STUFF, TABLET, CATTIE HOOSE KEY

36   Outdoor Adventure / July 1973

How to make a survival kit

All kinds of things can go wrong outdoors. You may get lost and have to spend a night in the wilds, or bad weather might strand you on the side of a mountain. You need a survival kit. This small tin can crammed with things to give vital SHELTER, WARMTH, FOOD and SOS SIGNALS. It is like a goal-keeper. After everything else has failed, it will save the situation.

Make your own survival kit

Design your own survival kit as shown. Squeeze the items into as small a tin as possible. Stick glo-coloured tape round to seal it tight. Keep it in your rucksack or pocket.

Big Plastic Bag (lightweight about 8 x 4 ft, 2.4 x 1.2 m), such as bags used by dry cleaners: You can sit out a night of bad weather in this as shown, with your feet in the rucksack. Bag must have hole in it to breathe through.
Waterproof matches.
Short length of candle.
String (strong and thin).
Wire (thick fuse wire, good for making snares for rabbits).
Small Stainless Steel Penknife: it must have large finger and thumb holes so it can easily be opened with wet, cold and muddy fingers.
Signalling Mirror.
Emergency Food: any kind which has a high

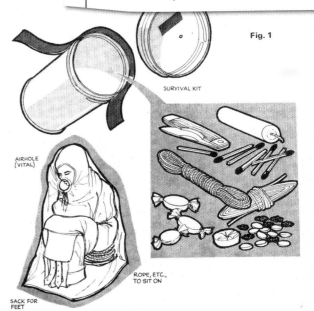

Fig. 1

SURVIVAL KIT

AIRHOLE (VITAL)

ROPE, ETC., TO SIT ON

SACK FOR FEET

energy content (like bits of Kendal mint cake, chocolate, nuts and raisins, dates or glucose tablets). You will not be able to carry much but every little helps until you have found some 'natural' food among the landscape.

When your survival kit runs out
The answer is: improvise. Make do with whatever else you have found around you.
This is survival.

Survivin' in the cauld

Weel, that's mair likely –
wha disnae like bein oot
in the cauld.

Here is the adventure
o' Wullie the Eskimo.

First I built an
igloo, an' I made a
grand job o' it.

Then I pit on ma
snow shoes tae go
tae the park.

I went tae catch some
fish (weel, o' course I
hae tae go fishin'!).

An' then I
settled doon
for the nicht.

Here's some advice aboot buildin' an igloo or a snow-hole. It's great tae imagine, but oor snow disnae last lang in Auchenshoogle. I didna manage tae stay the nicht in ma igloo, because it rained.

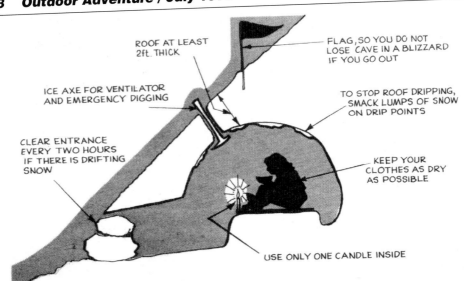

ROOF AT LEAST 2ft. THICK

FLAG, SO YOU DO NOT LOSE CAVE IN A BLIZZARD IF YOU GO OUT

ICE AXE FOR VENTILATOR AND EMERGENCY DIGGING

TO STOP ROOF DRIPPING, SMACK LUMPS OF SNOW ON DRIP POINTS

CLEAR ENTRANCE EVERY TWO HOURS IF THERE IS DRIFTING SNOW

KEEP YOUR CLOTHES AS DRY AS POSSIBLE

USE ONLY ONE CANDLE INSIDE

101 THINGS TAE DAE WI' A BUCKET

No. 23

SPLOSH!

WH

SPLOSH!

GOOD DEFENCE AGAINST SNOWBALL

Surviving in the Snow

Find a *big* snow-drift to dig your snow-hole in. Make it simple. Just burrow a hole big enough to get into. A small snow-hole will be warmer than a big one.

What do you dig with? A folding shovel if you have one, or a branch, a big bone, an ice axe or a rock. It will take about four hours for two of you to hack out a small cave as shown. The walls and roof should be at least 2 ft. (600 mm) thick. A freezing temperature is best to help 'cement' the roof so it does not collapse at once.

Channel into the snow bank tunnelling upwards. Scrape the snow out. Or, if hard enough, you can lift it out in blocks. Smooth the roof of the cave with a piece of branch or ice axe head so it does not drip. Carve out a 'bench' to sit on. Stamp the floor flat. Push a stick through the roof for ventilation (very important).

Living in the snow cave

It is much warmer than you think. Snow is an excellent insulator. Build up snow in the entrance once you are inside—leaving a small hole for air. Sit on a rucksack or a sweater or newspapers. Or cagoule. Do not wear *all* your clothes. *Keep everything dry.* And keep your axe inside in case the roof falls in and you have to dig yourself out.

Here's some mair survival tips for ye.

Survival Card (No.41)

Making a bed

● Lay out pine needles, dry moss, branches from evergreen trees, grass or heather for as thick and foamy a mattress as possible.

I tellt Fat Bob that holly wis an evergreen, so it would be guid for makin' a bed!

Survival Card (No.51)

Surviving lightning

● Safest places are in a car, a building (especially in a valley), the middle of a thick forest (but never under an isolated tree). Avoid steep ground, skylines, cliffs, rock faces, under overhangs, crowds of people on flat ground.

Presented with Outdoor Adventure Magazine

Survival Card (No.35)

Use snow as blotting paper

● If you fall into icy water, keep your clothes on when you get out. Roll over and over and over in the snow. This absorbs the moisture and the rolling makes you warm. Now and then jump up to bang off the snow.

Presented with Outdoor Adventure Magazine

Survival Card (No.33)

Smoke signals

● You need a good fire and a calm day. Use black smoke for gloomy days by burning bits of rubber, oily rags, etc.; white smoke on clear days by adding moss, green foliage, sprinkling the fire with urine.

Presented with Outdoor Adventure Magazine

I went campin' wi Pa – he didna like me pullin' faces (Big Feartie!!)

Survival Card (No.23)

Keeping warm

● Try to beat the shivers by wiggling your toes, slapping arms across your body, curling and uncurling fists, pushing your hands under your armpits; wear coat like a cape, buttoned up but no arms down sleeves. Jumping up and down with feet together, pulling faces (to avoid frostbitten cheeks) and pummeling a friend works wonders.

Presented with Outdoor Adventure Magazine

Survival Card (No.9)

Striking a match outside

● Strike the match into the wind. Slant the head into the 'cup' of your palms so the flame runs back up the stick if a draught gets through. Damp matches can be dried by rubbing gently in your hair.

Presented with Outdoor Adventure Magazine

Camouflage

I found a book aboot camouflage -"the art o' concealment by blending with the background". Jings! Whit a lot o' big words.

"The zebra uses its stripes tae look like long grass."
I'll draw stripes across masel' wi' white chalk.
Help ma boab! That wis nae guid.

Then I saw Fat Bob. Can I hide fae him? Easy!

Whit does the book say aboot a quick camouflage:
"The simplest forms o' camouflage are most effective. One man alone is distinctive. In a crowd he is unseen."

But it didna work. Ma spotted me (heard ma tacketty boots) and took me awa' hame.

108

Fishin'   Nuthin' tae it! Here's whit ye need:

A GOOD STICK, 4-5 ft (1.25 - 1.25 m) LONG
SOME STRING
A BENT NAIL
(AS THE HOOK)
BAIT
A RIVER
TIME
A BAG TAE CARRY FISH HAME IN

But fowk like tae mak' it mair complicated. In coarse fishin' ye catch fish ye wouldna want tae eat an' then throw them back intae the river. Fly fishin' or game fishin' is used tae catch fish tae eat. (Imagine no' eatin' yer catch! Some fowk are daft.)

COARSE FISH:
No very tasty!
BARBEL
GOLDEN BREAM
CHUB
DACE
PERCH
GED or PIKE
ROACH
RUDD
TENCH
GAME FISH:
These taste braw!
TROOT
SALMON
CHAR

AUCHENSHOOGLE POLICE STATION
DATE .....Saturday 15th.....
POLICE CONSTABLE .....Murdoch.....

Poaching is high on the list of priorities in local policing these days. It's called Wildlife Crime now. I have to keep a keen eye on things when the Gamekeeper has his day off. It makes a change from pounding the pavements once in a while, but I keep coming across the same culprits.

It's no' fair. Whit harm is it daein' tae catch a wee fishy? An' how come P.C. Murdoch's got nuthin' better tae dae than come doon by the river an' catch me? Should he no' be concentratin' on ither dangerous criminals?

But — I got ma ain back wi' a wee bit o' honest detective work, an' twa bob intae the bargain! Wha says poachin' disnae pay?

WULLIE'S WISDOMS

Sma' fish are better than nae fish at a'.

Here's a bit fae ane o' Pa's books tae tell ye mair aboot fishin'.

It has been said that in fishing there is a worm at one end of a line and a fool at the other. In many cases this may be true. But catching fish usually requires the angler to have his wits very much about him.

Whit a cheek!

EQUIPMENT

This, however limited, should be good of its kind. It is a very false economy to buy cheap lines, gut, and hooks, which will probably fail you when quality is most needed – when you have hooked a good fish. Also, take good care of your outfit; the very best soon deteriorates if neglected.

Dungarees are best!

GENERAL HINTS

Clothes should be of sober hue, as fishes have remarkably quick eyes. White flannels, though very comfortable on a hot day, are warranted to scare. Wear a grey or brown hat or cap.

Early morning and the evening are the best time for fishing; and a dull day is generally better than a sunny one.

Keep out of sight as much as possible; keep as quiet as possible; make as little splash as possible.

Give small fish the benefit of the doubt and throw them back.

When the water is muddy, fish feed in the shallows, where they can best see their food; when the water is clear, they generally move into deeper water.

Don't fish with the sun behind you if you can avoid it; shadows frighten fish.

The clearer the water, the finer the tackle should be.

I tried fly fishin' – an' I caught a' sorts o' things.

'You're making a rod for your own back.' Proves that Ma kens nuthin' aboot fishin'.

Cycling

I think cyclin' is ane o' the best things ever. Freedom! But ye hae tae learn aboot safety, when ye're on the roads, and that's aboot keepin' yer bike in guid nick so that the brakes work, and ye need tae ken aboot signallin' and the Highway Code. P.C. Murdoch does Cyclin' Proffishency testin' at the school playground an' ye get a badge. That's when Ma an' Pa said I could get my ain bike.

ABC of Bicycle Maintenance

ROAD MANNERS

The manner in which a bicycle is used, as well as the way in which it is kept, also proclaims the character of its owner. A bicycle is a vehicle. It has to obey the rules of the road just as have all the other vehicles.

Before a driver of a car is allowed to go alone on the public highway, he has to be tested and passed as efficient. How many young cyclists have even studied that booklet, which is one of the most important publications in the English language, the Highway Code?

One does not merely become a cyclist by being able to maintain one's balance and make the bicycle go. Before a cyclist goes out on to the road, he should know to keep to the left, how to make the necessary signals, how to make a right-hand turn (teen-agers run into more trouble while making this sometimes difficult manoeuvre than in any other way), know the traffic signs, know how to give way to pedestrians, especially at crossing-

places, and know the correct safety gear to wear, which must include a helmet. All this most vital information is set out in the Highway Code.

As well as telling us all about signs and signals, it tells us not to carry a passenger (unless the bicycle is specially fitted), not to carry parcels on the handlebars (fit a carrier, a saddle-bag or a basket), not to carry bulky loads, to keep the rear reflector clean and properly angled, and about the need for a rear light.

There are many road-users who disregard the Highway Code, who think they know better, who think they can take liberties and chances. This is a pity. They cause ninety-seven accidents out of one hundred. They are the spoil-sports.

Do not copy them in their silly ways. The real cyclist plays the game. His machine and his behaviour set an example to all. Along this way lie fun, happiness and fitness for those who follow one of the best of all outdoor pastimes.

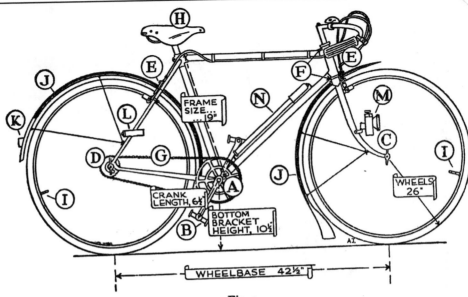

Fig. 3

A bicycle reflects the character of its owner. A clean, tidy, well-cared-for machine is one which will go far (as will its owner) and it will go with the minimum of bother and inconvenience.

Keeping a bicycle in good condition need not be a task. Overhaul it once, give it regular attention and the bicycle will repay in years of trouble-free service. Regular oiling, regular cleaning, the doing of odd jobs as they are needed, is the idea. Little and often is the secret of success.

A. Bottom Bracket : Lubricate frequently. Heavy oil is best. Should spin freely and without shake. Liable to be affected by water from spray of front wheel. This can cause crackling noise similar to that of broken ball-bearings.

B. Pedals: Heavy oil.

C. Front Hub: Adjust until free of shake. Weight of valve should be able to swing wheel. Heavy oil. Use duster to prevent oil travelling along spokes to tyres. (Oil is bad for rubber.)

D. Rear Hub: As for front hub. Lubricate free-wheel by laying bicycle on its side and spinning wheel to allow thin oil to work its way in.

E. Brakes: Oil where metal parts rub. Keep brake-shoes close to rim.

F. Steering Column: Avoid shake. Thin oil regularly.

G. Chain: Allow not more than one inch of up and down" play". Heavy oil to inside. See that chain-wheel bolts are tight.

H. Saddle: Keep dry. Oil if it creaks. Saddle top may be tightened by nut under peak.

I. Valve: Keep tight. Talc will allow you to slip on rubber replacements.

J. Mudguards: Do not allow to be loose.

K. Reflector: Keep clean and properly angled.

L. Rear Light: Red glass. Essential after lighting-up time.

M. Head Lamp: White. Focus to avoid dazzling other road-users. Carry spare bulbs, and batteries, if necessary.

N. Pump for tyres: An occasional spot of oil will keep washer pliable.

In General: Oil often but sparingly. Keep tyres inflated hard.

20

PART 6 - Ma nature book

I like spring time. It's a chance tae get ootdoors again efter the winter. But I like summer even mair!

Spring - A Poem by Wullie

The springtime air so fresh an' pure,
Is often spoilt by housewives' stour.

Young lambs are gambolin' a' the day. I saw some men, they were gamblin' tae.

The little birdie builds her nest, But climbin' trees gies breeks a test.

The daffodils make my young heart gled, But I left mine below the bed.

Really spring is just a scunner, It's high time that it turned tae summer.

1. Jay.
2. Great Bird of Paradise.
3. Rosy Starling.
4. Java Sparrow.
5. Violet Tanager; male and female.
6. Scarlet Rose Finch; male and female.
7. Chinese Lark.
8. White Wagtail.
9. Nuthatch.
10. Red-backed Shrike; male and female.
11. Waxwing.
12. Reed Warbler.
13. White-winged Black Bulbul.
14. Lyre Bird; male and female.
15. Spotted Woodpecker.
16. Toucan.
17. Fork-tailed Humming Bird; male and female.
18. Racket-tailed Humming Bird.
19. Swift.
20. Kingfisher.
21. Yellow and Blue Macaw.
22. Parroquet.
23. Tawny Owl.
24. Osprey.
25. Golden Eagle.
26. Ruppell's Vulture.
27. Secretary Bird.
28. Pelican.
29. Flamingo.
30. Sacred Ibis.
31. Stanley Crane.
32. Razorbill.
33. Albatross.
34. Red-throated Diver in summer and winter plumage.
35. Victoria Crowned Pigeon.
36. Ptarmigan in summer and winter plumage.
37. Chinese Pheasant; male and female.
38. Ostrich.
39. Kiwi.

S.T.DADD

A few birds ye cannae see aroond Auchenshoogle.

WULLIE'S WISDOMS

A bird in the hand is worth two in the bush.

Chaffinch

Birds

The maist common gairden birds in Scotland.

Robin

Great Tit

Blackbird

Sparrow

1	CHAFFINCH	Tae help
2	HOUSE SPARROW	the birds,
3	STARLING	ye can
4	BLUE TIT	feed them.
5	BLACKBIRD	Here's
6	GREENFINCH	some richt
7	GREAT TIT	guid advice. →
8	ROBIN	
9	DUNNOCK	Ither
10	GOLDFINCH	birds ye may see.

Cuckoo

Feed the birds

● Put a bird table in part of the garden where the birds can use it without being frightened, but where you can easily watch it from a distance without being seen. Ideally you should be able to see the table from a room in the house, so that you can watch the birds from inside during the winter. You may have to try putting it in several different parts of your garden before you find one which the birds really trust.

See if you can train birds to come to the table at certain feeding times, always putting new food on the table at the same time each day.

Feeding tips
Birds are not the only animals that would like to eat the food you put out, so:
● Don't put food on the ground or low down. It will attract mice and rats.
● Make sure any food dropped from the table is cleared up.
● Place the table in a position that cats cannot jump on to it. Avoid placing the table close to bushes unless it is a holly bush or some other equally prickly plant.
● Grey squirrels are great climbers, and preventing then getting onto the bird table will challenge your ingenuity Place baffles on the stake to stop squirrels climbing up.

What to feed birds

● Seed mixes There are lots of bird seed mixtures available. Avoid mixes that contain split peas, beans or dried rice as only larger birds will eat them. Some good seeds are: millet seeds, sunflower seeds, flaked maize, pinhead oatmeal.
● Peanuts and crushed peanuts (but not dry roasted or salted).
● Nyjer seeds require a special feeder. Popular with goldfinches and siskins.
● Wheat and barley grains only really suitable for large, ground-eating birds – pigeons, doves and pheasants. Their presence will frighten off other birds.
● Fat balls, especially in winter. You can buy them or make them: Pour melted suet or lard onto a mixture of seeds, nuts, fried fruit oatmeal (plus cheese or cake), about one third-fat, two-thirds mixture. Mix well and leave to set in a container of your choice.
● Live mealworms are popular with robins and blue tits. You can buy them or rear them yourself. (The RSPB can advise on how do to this.)
● Don't put out milk, margarine, vegetable oils, desiccated coconut, cooked porridge oats, mouldy or stale food or dry biscuits

Barn Owl

Skylark

Crow

Ma bird world

I hae tae find oot aboot birds for homework. There are some richt odd birds aroond.

The noisiest bird: There's a parrot in New Zealand ca'd the Kakapo. It's muckle an' canna fly but it mak's a noise like a fog horn that can be heard 3 miles (5 km) awa'.

The fastest bird: I'd run hame tae catch Ma's mince an' tatties, but the peregrine falcon can go at 200 miles an hour (322 k.p.h) tae catch its food. It's the fastest animal in the world.

Scotland's biggest bird: Well, it isnae the golden eagle, it's the sea eagle (no, I dinnae mean seagull). Its wingspan can be uptae 8 ft. (250 cm). They like tae eat animals that are a'ready deid – they've been seen eatin' rabbits, hares, deer, sheep, gulls, geese an' swans (but nae chips!). No' picky then.

BIRD FACTS

The largest wingspan

The bird with the biggest wings is the wandering albatross, up to 11 ft. (3.4 m) long. They can live for 50 years and their favourite food is deep-water squid.

The biggest bird

The ostrich is a bird that cannot fly but it's a record breaker – it's the tallest bird, the heaviest bird, the fastest runner, produces the largest egg and has the biggest eye of any bird. It can be up to 9 ft. (2.8 m) tall and can run at 45 miles per hour (72 k.p.h).

Long-distance flying

In its first two years the swift never settles on the ground. In that time it flies almost the distance to the moon and back. Later, when feeding its young it can fly 600 miles (960 km) a day.

Floo'ers

Dandelions are the best!
Then Sweet Williams, o' course!

Ye can mak' braw noises
wi' the stalks o' dandelions.

An' a secret is worth the twa bob that Granpaw Broon gied
me. But as ye hae paid for ma book, ye can hav' the secret
for nuthin'. But dinna read on if ye havnae paid!

WULLIE'S DANDELION SECRET

TAE MAK' A NOISE WI'
A DANDELION STALK:
SLIT ONE END O' THE STALK.
THEN BLOW THOUGH IT.
THIS IS WHIT MAKES
THE NOISE.

Jings, both Ma and Granpaw Broon are happy. Guid job done.	Ma likes floo'ers, an' she really likes bein' given them. Remember that for yer ain ma's birthdays! I dinna think Ma wanted dandelions, so I bocht same floo'ers fae a shop.	Ma favourite floo'ers Dandelion Sweet William Thistle Venus Fly Trap

Funny floo'ers: The biggest floo'er in the world disnae grow aboot
here but in the jungle. It's MASSIVE. It's aboot 3 ft. (900 mm)
across. But it isnae pretty an' it stinks o' rotten meat, so
dinna gie Rafflesia (that's its name) as a gift!

Plants ye can eat
There's free food oot in the country if ye ken whit tae look for.

Wullie's
Fund-Raising Scheme
Ask a fairmer if ye
can help pick his
fruit, but I hope ye
dae better than me
an' Fat Bob.

GREAT
BRITISH
FRUIT

BLACKBERRY

Wullie's Warnin'
DINNA PICK MUSHROOMS.
SOME ARE POISONOUS
DINNA PICK FRUIT FAE
ITHER FOWK'S GAIRDENS
(LEAVE IT FOR ME)

BEST WILD
FRUIT
BLACKBERRIES
RASPBERRIES
APPLES
HAZEL NUTS
BILBERRIES
WILD PLUMS

"The best things in life are free." I said that
tae Mrs McIvor at the sweetie shop - Ma
had said it wis ok . . . I still got a belt roond
the lug.

Ways tae pick apples

1. Use a fishin' net, but dinna collect ower many apples.

2. Try an arrow wi' a sucker on a lang string.

SNAP

3. Sneak in when naebody's aboot but beware o' dugs.

GET THE IDEA? I'LL RING THE BELL AND HIDE...

WEDGE

...THEN WHEN MURDOCH OPENS THE DOOR THE CARTIE WILL RUN AWA'...

IT'S WULLIE ON HIS CARTIE!

...AND WHEN HE CHASES THE DUMMY, I'LL NIP IN AND HELP MYSEL'.

4. Try this scheme! But why did I try it wi' P.C. Murdoch?

Once P.C. Murdoch gave me a tray o' apples. It wasnae the same as pinchin' them.

GREAT BRITISH FRUIT

APPLES

ONYBODY WANT AN APPLE?

Ma Gairdenin' Year

January
Put oot some food an' water for the birds tae scoff. Mak' sure the water isnae frozen – birds dinnae like skatin'.

February
Check on the pond an' add some mair water, usin' a bucket, o' course.

May
Plant seed for floo'ers an' veg.

June
Get oot an' water the plants – believe me, it's the driest month o' the year.

July
Enjoy the gairden – it's magic!

March
Bring oot the bulbs fae under the bed afore it's ower late.

April
Get Soapy an' Wee Eck tae check the nestin' boxes for blue tits.

August
Eat yer piece in the gairden an' watch the flutterbies.

September
Try gatherin' some wild floo'er seeds. Pa said something aboot sowin' wild oats but I didna follow it.

October
Plant some bulbs for floo'ers next spring.

November
Time tae plant trees, but no' close to any buildin' cos they grow ENORMOUS.

December
Put yer feet up - but put up nestin' boxes an' a'.

Trees

I heard the auld sayin' "You cannae see the wood for the trees." O' course ye can. Trees are made o' wid!

Here are some drawin's o' trees, done a' fancy. I should hae added some o' my ane.

Trees

Trees are the largest living things on earth. They are plants which draw in water, through their roots, and use their leaves as factories to make and store the food which they need for life. They divide into two very distinct categories – evergreen and deciduous.

Evergreens

As the name suggests, evergreen trees always have a covering of leaves. In winter they are the trees with leaves on them.

Deciduous trees

Deciduous trees lose their leaves every winter and grow a fresh set every spring. During the winter months, a deciduous tree looks stark and dead.

Each type of tree has different features. Here are two ways you can record that difference.

Bark rubbing

You will need some sheets of stout paper, ideally A3 size. Cartridge paper is good for this activity. You will also need a thick black wax crayon.

Choose as smooth an area of bark as you can find on your selected tree, and pin down the sheet of paper. Ask a friend to hold the paper steady for you. It is important that the paper does not move while you are making the rubbing. Gently

TREE – CHESTNUT (DECIDUOUS)

begin to shade over the whole area with the crayon or wax. Do not try to get a strong black result with your first strokes. If you do you may damage the paper. Take it easy at the beginning, and you will find you can go over the whole area time after time, until you have a fine drawing of the bark of your tree.

Leaf rubbing

When leaf rubbing you must be more careful and use a finer type of paper. Pla the leaf you have chosen carefully under a sheet of writing paper and, using a sof pencil, rub carefully over the whole area until the pattern of the veins begins to appear.

The oldest and tallest trees in Britain

The oldest tree in Britain (and probably Europe) is a yew by the kirk at Fortingall, near Aberfeldy in Perthshire. It is estimated to be between 2,500 and 5,000 years old. Its trunk had a girth of 52 ft in 1769, although this is now less obvious to see as the surviving growth is around the edge of the tree and all the wood has vanished from its centre. It is a local tradition that Pontius Pilate was born nearby and may have played in the shadow of the yew.

The tallest tree in Britain is the Stronardon Douglas fir near Dunans Castle in Argyll, coming in at 209 ft. tall – that's about 40 ft. taller than Nelson's Column in Trafalgar Square in London.

ASH   HORSE CHESTNUT   LIME
ALDER   WILLOW   OAK   LARCH
SYCAMORE   BEECH   CHESTNUT

ROWAN   FIELD MAPLE   HAZEL
PLANE   WALNUT   ELM
CEDAR   POPLAR   BIRCH   SCOTS PINE   SPRUCE

Ma favourite tree is the Horse chestnut. It gies us CONKERS!!!

Creepy crawlies

Ma favoorites – there are lots aroond an' ye can dae a' sorts o' things wi' them – ye can keep them an' watch them grow – an' they're great for givin' Primrose a fleg.

INSECTS
THAT BITE
MIDGIES
CLEGS
WASPS
MOSQUITOES
SCORPIONS
GNATS
BLACK WIDOW
SPIDER
BEES
ANTS

FRIENDLY
INSECTS
LADYBIRDS
CATERPILLARS
DRAGONFLIES
GRASSHOPPERS
STICK INSECTS
BUTTERFLIES
MOTHS (BUT MA
SAYS THEY EAT
CLAES)

Fat Bob and Soapy sat on some anthills when we campe Ma bucket kept me safe.

Butterflies

I've coloured in a bonnie butterfly. Ye can dae the ither twa. Whit dae ye think o' mine?

PROJECTS

Rearing small tortoiseshell caterpillars

Small tortoiseshell butterflies are common in most parts of the country. They are easy to rear and grow quickly. You will not have to wait through the winter for them to hatch.

The picture shows the four stages of the life cycle of the small tortoiseshell. The caterpillars only feed on stinging nettles. If you have seen the butterflies in your garden and know there is a good nettle patch close to your house, then you will know this is where the caterpillars are.

It is best to start with the small caterpillars which you can find in late May or early June and in August. As long as possible before collecting your caterpillars make some arrangements to house and feed them. You can make caterpillar cages from old shoe boxes. Cut out the centre of the lid, leaving ½ in (12.5 mm) all round. Stick some transparent plastic over the hole with sticky tape.

Dig up and plant some nettle plants in small flower pots. Choose the pots and plants so that they will fit into your cage.

Now you are ready to find some caterpillars. Look for leaves at the tops of nettle plants which have been covered in a silken tent. In or on this tent will be large numbers of small caterpillars. You may have to search for a long time before you find any. If you find none, try again a bit later in the year. The time when caterpillars are small varies in different parts of the country. Do not collect too many caterpillars. It is easy to feed hundreds of small caterpillars, but they will soon grow and eat so much you will run out of potted nettle plants. Take about

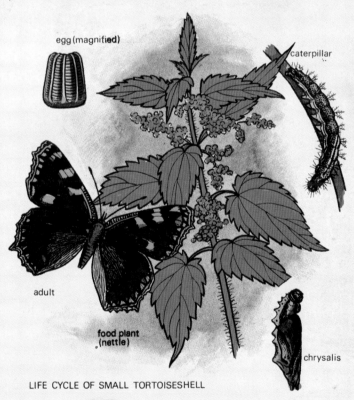

LIFE CYCLE OF SMALL TORTOISESHELL

20 small caterpillars on a leaf of nettle. Pick it up carefully so you will not get stung. Do not try to move the caterpillars off their leaf. Just put the leaf on the growing plant in the cage and the caterpillars will soon crawl on to the new plant and start to spin themselves a new silk tent

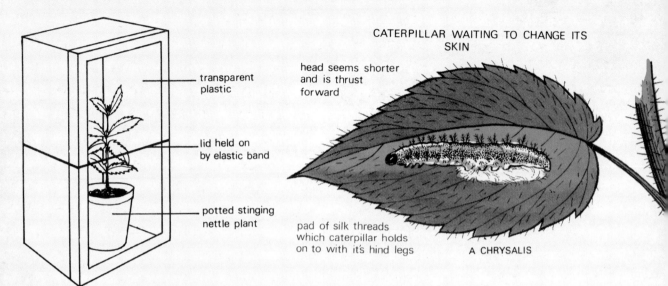

transparent
plastic

lid held on
by elastic band

potted stinging
nettle plant

CATERPILLAR WAITING TO CHANGE ITS
SKIN

head seems shorter
and is thrust
forward

pad of silk threads
which caterpillar holds
on to with it's hind legs

A CHRYSALIS

Rearing small tortoiseshell caterpillars
Continued

Within a few days you will probably notice some which seem
to be ill. They stop feeding and sit on a silk pad they have spun
on the leaf. There is a pad of silk threads which the caterpillar
will hold on to with its hind legs. This is in preparation for
changing its skin. While it is resting the new skin is being
completed underneath the old one. When it is ready, the old
skin splits behind the head and the caterpillar crawls out of its
old skin. When the new skin has hardened, the caterpillar will
start to eat again.

Turning into a chrysalis

While the caterpillars are feeding and growing they will not
leave the nettle plant unless all the leaves have been eaten. As
long as you put a new plant in besides the old plant before
it is entirely eaten, the caterpillars will not try to escape. But
when the caterpillars are fully grown, they will wander away
from the plant and crawl up the sides of the box. Here they
will spin a silken pad and hang, with head curled round and
the body getting shorter and fatter. Hanging up like this the
caterpillar will change its skin for the last time and turn into a
chrysalis.

Watch carefully how it does this without letting go and
falling down. It starts light coloured and very soft, but it soon
hardens and darkens. If you touch it while it is still soft, it may
be damaged and die.

When the chrysalis has hardened (after a day it will be safe)

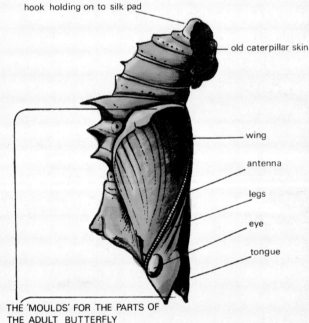

hook holding on to silk pad

old caterpillar skin

wing

antenna

legs

eye

tongue

THE 'MOULDS' FOR THE PARTS OF
THE ADULT BUTTERFLY

take a close look at it. You will see it is shaped as if it were a
mould for a butterfly.

Look at the chrysalis each day. A day or two before it hatches,
will change colour again. The wing cover will become transpare
and you will be able to see tiny wings inside the chrysalis. Now
comes the most exciting stage and you will be lucky to see it
happening. The butterfly crawls up the old case and hangs from
the side or top of the box. Its body is fully sized but the wings
are small and flabby. Gradually the wings stretch until they reac
full size. They then begin to harden and after about an hour, the
butterfly is ready for its first flight. What a transformation!

Wullie's Fund-Raisin' Scheme

People a'ways like lookin' at odd things in nature. If ye show something richt strange, they'll pay ye tae see it. Whit can go wrang!

Mrs Bell gied me a magnifyin' glass for daeing her messages.

I'm nae guid as a detective so I had an idea for usin' the magnifyin' glass. I cut a hole in the end o' a shoe box...

Soon I wis takin' in money. A'body started pushin' tae see ma monster o' a snake.

I wis too late tae stop the box fallin' ower. Oot o' it tumbled a worm and a magnifyin' glass.

Time for a quick exit, but they still caught me in the park. So much for makin' money!

129

PART 7 - Sports an' games
Fitba

I fancy masel' kickin' a fitba' aboot.

It would be even better if the kitchen windie wisnae there...

I wis once picked for the toffee-nosed Laurel Avenue team. Trouble wis I had nae kit o' my ain an' had tae borrow Hen Broon's - whit a picture I made.

I'm goin' tae let ye intae my secret ways o' watchin' a fitba' match wi'out payin'. All guaranteed foolproof, o' course.

1. Practise trick cycling.

2. Tryin' tae sneak in (but this didna work)

3. Dress in fitba' kit an' pretend tae be a ball boy.

4. Be the team mascot (no' recommended).

5. Kicking my fitba intae the ground when the match ba' is kicked oot.

101 THINGS TAE DAE WI' A BUCKET No. 4

STAND ON IT TO SEE OVER THE FENCE AT THE BIG FOOTY MATCH

Fechtin'

Whit I dinna understand is that we sit learnin' aboot History which is a' aboot fechtin' that's been goin' on for hunners o' years, but when I get intae trouble, an' P.C. Murdoch gies me a richt tellin' aff, Ma and Pa go daft an' the teacher keeps me back at the end o' the day, an' I hae tae write aboot Anger Manaigement.
Whit am I supposed tae dae? Turn the ither cheek? Aye that'll be richt!

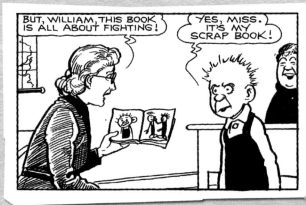

Ma disnae like boxin' - so I tellt her that I wis daein' Marshall Arts.
"Whit kind o' Marshall Arts?" she says.
"Tai-Foo."
"Whit's that?" she says.
"It's a cross between Tai Kwandoh an' Kung Fu, an' we've got cups for it!"

4. Buffalo Bill Meets Yellow Hand.

6. Ned Kelly's Last Stand.

THE WIZARD ALBUM OF FAMOUS FIGHTS

Need tae think up ma nickname.
A' the top boxers hae a name.
Jack Johnson wis the Galveston Giant.
Jack Dempsey's nickname wis the Manassa Mauler.
Mike Tyson's nickname wis Iron.

George Foreman's nickname wis Big.

Evander Holyfield's nickname wis Real Deal.
James Corbett wis known as Gentleman Jim.
I think I should be the Auchenshoogle Basher.

3. Jack Dempsey v. Gene Tunney.

Body buildin'

We had a talk fae an athletic athlete at the school, and we asked him aboot body buildin' an' fitness an' trainin'. He said you need a high protein diet – tae eat enough protein so yer body is able tae build lean muscle mass. He said a'body's body is different and develops in different ways at different ages. Its yer jeans!

But whit if ye hae dungarees?

Egg white, fish, meat, beef, chicken an' turkey gie ye the best protein.

Next ye need a trainer at the gym – a proper trainer who knows what he is daein' so ye get proper workouts that suit ye, which is when the hard work starts.

think I'll just dae the first bit. Eat a mass o' lean mince. I'll leave the gym trainin' for a bit. It's exercise enuff wi' fitba', swimmin', cyclin' an' runnin' awa' fae P.C. Murdoch!

"*I'll prove in only 7 days I can make* **YOU a NEW MAN**"

No other Physical Instructor has ever DARED make such an offer

By CHARLES ATLAS
Holder of the Title:
"*The World's Most Perfectly Developed Man*"

YOU don't have to take *my* word —nor that of hundreds of my pupils who have added inches to their chests, biceps, necks, thighs and calves. Prove *for yourself* in just one week that you can, too, actually become a husky, healthy, NEW MAN!

My *Dynamic Tension* system does it. That's how I built myself up from a 97-pound weakling to "The World's Most Perfectly Developed Man." Let me prove that you can get balanced muscular development the same easy way.

Gamble a Stamp
Coupon for FREE

Dynamic Tension is a natural method of developing you, inside and out, without using any pills, unnatural tricky weights or pulleys that strain your heart or other vital organs, causing such ailments as constipation, pimples, blotches, and other conditions that keep you from really enjoying life.

Gamble a stamp today. Mail for a free copy of my new book. "Everlasting Health and Strength." It shows, from actual photos, how I developed my pupils to the perfectly balanced proportions of my own body.

Jot your name and address on the coupon. Send it to me personally. CHARLES ATLAS, Dept. 63, 115 East 23rd Street, New York, N. Y.

CHARLES ATLAS, Dept. 63,
115 East 23rd Street, New York, N. Y.

I want the proof that your system of *Dynamic Tension* will make a New Man of me—give me a healthy, husky body. Send me your free book.

Name ....
(Please print or write plainly)

Address ....

WULLIE'S WISDOMS

If it's ower good tae be true, then it probably is.

Commonwealth Games

Guess whit! I've just seen in the paper that the Commonwealth Games is comin' tae Glasgow! It's the XXth. (That's Roman numbers, X is ten, so XX is twenty).

The Games is in 2014, and they're needin' finely tuned athletes tae get trainin'. I'm goin' tae get Fat Bob an' Soapy an' Wee Eck an' me superfit an' in shape for the Games, an' it's ideal that we've got the school sports comin' up tae practice.

Whit are we best at?
Egg and Spoon race? Sack Race?

But they dae shootin' as weel at the Commonwealth Games - better than oor Sports Day! Mebbe I could be the Catapult champion

I could dae Airchie Rae - bows an' arras an' fixed targets - easy peasy.
Or Boxin' - boxin's just fechtin' wi' gloves on! Or mebbe I can dae the swimmin' an' divin'?

WULLIE'S WISDOMS

Winning isn't everything. It's the only thing!

Cyclin' - I could be like Chris Hoy. I'd need a new bell on ma bike, and racin' handlebars, an' a go faster hat wi' a pointy bit at the back.

Wullie's Trainin' Tips
Egg and Spoon Race
technique
The secret wi' the egg
an' spoon race is tae pit
yer thumb on the egg. No'
richt on the top, but just
steady it at the thin end
– go slowly tae begin – wi'
yer tongue oot like ye're
concentratin' then get up
tae a gallop – nae bother!

The start of the
Auchenshoogle Marathon

Whit a funny
sport!

Cricket should be at the Games
as weel – a' ye need tae ken:

There's twa sides – ane oot in
the field an' ane in.

Each man that's in the side
that goes in goes oot an' when
he's oot he comes in an' the
next man goes in until he's oot..

When they are a' oot the side that's oot
comes in an' the side that's been in goes
oot an' tries tae get those comin' in oot..

When both sides hae been in an' oot
includin' not oots, that's the end o' the
game.
      Simple!

137

Hielan' Games

THE CABER TOSS

The Hielan' Games isnae jist aboot athletical stuff.

There's loads o' kilties playing bagpipes, and drummers drummin' an' dancers daein' the hielan' fling, fiddlers fiddlin' and strong men tossin' cabers the size o' telegraph poles.

THE STONE TOSS

There's hammer throwers an' shot puttin' (like on the porridge box, no' the puttin' green beside the swings).

P.C. Murdoch says in aulden times the Chiefs o' a' the clans would make their men dae feats o' strength tae prove themselves as bonnie fechters.

The Tug-o'-War is oor favoorite. You need a long thick rope wi' a centre mark and a mark at the head o' each team, an' a mark on the ground. When the call comes tae "heave" each team tries tae pull the ither ower the centre line.

WULLIE'S WISDOMS

Nae wonder us Scots fowk hae a sense of humour – it's free !

There's usually sheep herding wi' Border Collies (like Black Bob fae The Dandy) and their shepherds who can whistle tae tell their dugs whit tae dae. These are clever dugs !

There's Scottish Hielan games
a' ower the world !

138

THE STONE TOSS

Ma friends were a' dancin' at the Games.

But I still got a turn.

HIGHLAND DANCING

A' because a wasp stung me – an' the judge gied me twa bob!

Pa tellt me that P.C. Murdoch wis a braw athlete when he wis young. He used tae toss the caber an' throw the hammer. I'm glad he wis never a runner – he might catch me then! Jings, whit a man! I asked him if he wud teach us a' aboot Hielan' sports.

It looked simple when he showed us.

But we didnae find it so easy!

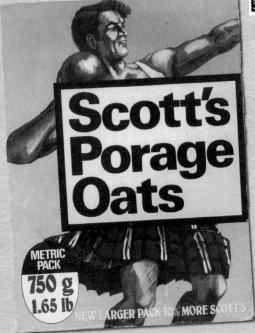

That wis the end o' oor trainin' for the Hielan' Games!

Acrobatics

The circus is in town! I fancy bein' an acrobat – but I'll need tae practise.

I practise at the swing park. A' Fat Bob can dae is sit on the swings, but I am skilled wi' the rings.

When a wee laddie said I wis nae guid, I bet him a shillin' he couldna dae better. I shouldna hae bothered.

I lost ma bet an' had nae money for the circus. Fat Bob got his ticket. I jist walked ootside the tent until . . .

Weel, sittin' doon is a lot easier than bein' an acrobat!

PART 8 –
Makin' music

Here are some braw ways tae mak' yer ain music. Ye'll ken that it sounds beautiful. Dinnae believe anybody that says they dinnae like it.

Making musical sounds

The easiest musical sound you can make is by clapping your hands. When men still lived in caves they made simple music by shouting, clapping, beating their chests and stamping their feet. Spanish dancers clap their hands and tap their feet; Russians slap their knees and thighs when they dance; and we use our voices for singing. But some of the most exciting sounds are made with musical instruments. A quick look at home will help you with your first musical sounds. Look for:

- a comb
- a piece of tissue paper
- a wooden spoon
- a saucepan
- two sticks
- an elastic band

Four ways to make sounds
Here are four ways of making musical sounds:

- blowing
- plucking
- hitting
- rubbing

Blowing. Blow to make a sound like the wind or whistle through your teeth. Play tunes by blowing on a piece of tissue paper over a comb.

Plucking. Make a plucking sound by putting your finger in your cheek and pulling it out quickly. Stretch an elastic band from a doorknob and pluck it.

Hitting. Clap your hands. Use different parts of your hands to make loud and soft sounds. A wooden spoon on a can or saucepan (upside down) makes a drumming sound.

Rubbing. Rub your feet on the floor. Rub two sticks together and you have two rhythm sticks.

Aye, that's music tae ma ears.
I'll away and mak' some new tunes. Ma will love them . . .

Making a tune

Try 'Three Blind Mice'. One person plays the tune on the comb and paper while the rest use the spoon and saucepan, elastic band and sticks, as well as finger-in-cheek sounds and clapping. By the side of each line you will see what to do. You will have to practice it a few times first so that you know exactly when to play your parts. You can sing as well!

Fairly softly, keep time with spoon and saucepan.	**Three blind mice!**	End the line with three twangs on the elastic band.
Repeat louder.	**Three blind mice!**	Repeat louder.
Rub sticks quickly for the sound of mice running.	**See how they run!**	Three handclaps.
Repeat louder.	**See how they run!**	Three beats on the saucepan.
Fairly loudly, use saucepan and elastic to keep time.	**They all ran after the farmer's wife,**	Popping sound in cheek.
Very loudly, repeat	**Who cut off their tails with a carving knife!**	Three beats on saucepan for tails being cut off
Softly twang elastic band.	**Did you ever see such a thing in your life**	Popping sound with finger in cheek
Loudly beat on saucepan.	**As three blind mice?**	Three loud beats on saucepan and three loud handclaps.

Ma Uncle Albert took me tae a symfunny concert.
It wis rare – they'd a' got queer instruments – an' they
were jist blawin' their heids aff. The wee man wi' the
stick wisna a bad contorshunist!

Fat Bob thocht we should mak' oor ain musical instruments, then we could gie a symfunny concert! Here are a few wee ideas.

MAKING MUSICAL INSTRUMENTS

BOTTLE PERCUSSION

You can play a tune on eight bottles. You can also use glasses or glass jars.
• Stand the bottles in a row.
• Strike one bottle with a spoon. It makes a clear note. You should be able to hum it. Leave this bottle as it is. Label it number eight.
• Fill the next bottle until when you hit it, it will hum the next note down. This is bottle number seven.
• Fill the next bottle, until it gives you the third note down and so on.
• Your eighth bottle should be full of water and this will be number one.

When your eight bottles are labelled try and play this tune:

```
3   3   4   4   5   6   7   6   5;
    4   4   3   3   2   2   1;
    4   4   4   3   3   2   2   2   1;
5   5   4   5   6   5   4   4   3   3   2.
```

See what sound you make if you hit two bottles at the same time.

PLANT POT MUSIC

This would drive Ma an' Pa "potty"! I hae tae mak' ane!

If you take a few pot plants of different sizes, a stick or broom handle, a piece of string, a cotton reel, and a hook for each pot, you can make plant pot bells.
• Do not try too hard to get plant pots that go up equally in size.
• Screw the hooks on different sides of the stick or broom handle with plenty of space below and above to give room for the bells to hang.
• Tie each piece of string through a cotton reel and tie a large knot in one end, so that it cannot slip through the reel.
• Thread the other end of the string through the hole in the bottom of the pot and tie it round the hook.
• The bells will hang down and you can strike them with a stick.
• You can number the pots in the same way as you numbered the bottles so that you can write down the tunes you play on them.

MAKING MUSICAL INSTRUMENTS

ELASTIC GUITARS

You can make guitars very easily with a few things; just a cardboard box and elastic bands, each ¼ in. (6 mm) thick.

• Take your cardboard box and make marks every ½ in. (12.5 mm) along the side of the box, as shown.

• The number of marks will depend on the size of your box.

• Leave the first mark as it is.

• Make a ¼ in. (6 mm) cut in the side of the box at the second mark and a ½ in. (12.5 mm) cut at the third mark, and so on.

• Now stretch a band over each mark and you will find that the deeper the cut in the box, the lower the note the elastic will make when it is plucked.

To tone your guitar, you can use your cardboard box again, but this time use elastic bands of different sizes.

• Stretch the elastic bands in order of size over the box.

• The difference in the size of the elastic bands will give you the difference in tone.

Alternatively, you could cut a triangular shape out of the

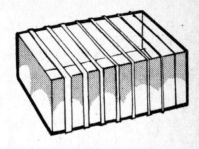

cardboard and also three strips for the sides as shown. Use strong glue to stick them. Stretch the elastic bands in order of size.

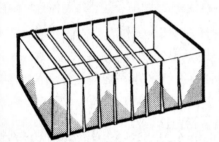

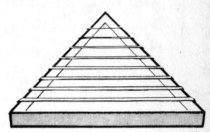

SHAKERS

To make any shaker you can use a jar with a screw top, a small box, or two yoghurt cartons; and something which will rattle inside, for example, split peas, coffee beans, rice or small pieces of gravel.

• Half fill the container with the filling of your choice.

• Fix the lid firmly on.

• If you are using yoghurt pots, fill up one side and stick the other on to it with glue.

• You can make shakers with different sounds by using different fillings.

TAMBOURINES

For tambourines you need a piece of cardboard 9 in. x 9 in. (225 x 225 mm), a pair of compasses, a collection of aluminium foil circles (milk bottle tops are ideal if you can find any), some thread and a needle.

• Make a circle as large as you can on the cardboard, using the pair of compasses, and then cut it out.

• Thread the milk bottle tops, attaching them loosely in groups of two or three around the edge of the cardboard circle.

• Shake this and you have a good rhythm instrument.

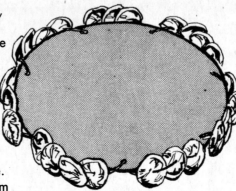

COAT-HANGER TRIANGLE

To make a triangle you will need two or three wire coat-hangers, and a piece of string.

• Bend the coat hangers to make them slightly fatter than before.

• Tie them by their hooks on to a piece of string, so that they dangle freely.

• Hit them with a spoon in time to the music.

MAKING MUSICAL INSTRUMENTS

A WOOD PIECE XYLOPHONE

Take any flat pieces of wood that you can find of different sizes, a flat piece of plastic foam and a stick to strike with.
• Put the pieces of wood on the foam.
• Strike them and find out which ones are the lowest and which the highest.

• Place them in order, beginning with the lowest notes.
• See if you can play a simple tune on it.

RHYTHM STICKS

For these you only need two sticks. Rubbed together they will make a swishing sound. If you cut notches with a penknife along the side of one stick, you will make a rough, rasping sound when you rub the two sticks together.

YOGHURT PERCUSSION

Take eight yoghurt pots (or eight paper or plastic cups), one piece of balsa wood 22 in. x 4 in. (550 x 100 mm), one tube of strong glue, and a piece of wood for a drumstick.
• Sandpaper the balsa wood so that it is smooth.
• Leave one carton as it is.
• From the second carton, cut off 2/5 in. (10 mm) with a fine hacksaw.
• With the third cup, cut 4/5 in. (20 mm) off.
• With the fourth cut off 30 mm and so on until you have cut off 70 mm from the eighth carton.

• Place the eight cartons in order of height on the balsa wood, so that there is the same amount of space between each one.
• Draw around the bases in pencil.
• Then glue them back in the same positions.
• Paint the cartons (or cups) and the wood base.
• Sandpaper both ends of the drumstick so that they are rounded.

MAKING RHYTHMS

If you listen carefully you will hear rhythms all around you. See if you can beat out these rhythms: soldiers marching, rabbits hopping, children running, rain falling, a horse galloping. Can you think of other rhythms you can make?

Rhythm can also give you a feeling of atmosphere. It can calm you down or make you feel very excited. Use rhythm to make this story exiting.

The rain fell softly makin' the street seem dour and empty.
Tap lightly on yoghurt carton for rain.
A man walked quietly alang the shadows of the hoose.
Footsteps.
He stopped at the house on the corner and the rain fell harder.
Tap louder.
He opened the garden gate and walked towards the window at the back.
Drum on saucepan lid slowly, but gradually getting faster.
Suddenly he hears a thud behind him.
Yoghurt carton.
Then another and another and his hearts beats faster.
Rub sticks together for heart beats.
He saw someone running towards him.
Make your own noises and finish the tale . . .

I didna half scare Wee Eck wi' ma tellin' o' that tale . . .

Wi' some o' these ideas an' some o' oor ain, we formed oor orchestra.

We found loads o' instruments, an' surely naebody would mind us bein' artistic!

We made braw music, but naebody else thocht so.

Anither place tae find musical instruments is in yer favoorite comic.

Here's ma favoorite squeaky balloon – but Ma dinna like it.

147

I dinna like goin' tae ma music lessons. They're a waste o' ma valuable time. I thocht aboot losing the violin, but it wis braw in a fecht. Whit better than giein' it tae the "weapons amnesty" o' P.C. Murdoch. He didnae ken whit tae say an' I missed ma lesson!

AUCHENSHOOGLE POLICE STATION
DATE Monday 14th
POLICE CONSTABLE Murdoch

HQ says I need to have a dangerous weapons register. There's to be an Amnesty. So if folk have got any dangerous weapons, now's their chance to turn them in, and they'll not get into any bother. What I didn't expect to be turned-in as a dangerous weapon was a violin. Guess who brought it?

But ma best music machine has tae be ma moothie.

An' I can play the bagpipes as weel!

149

Anither musical instrument ye can mak' for free is the squealer - a' ye need is a blade o' grass, an' ye can mak' a rare sound. No' a'body likes it though, so beware!

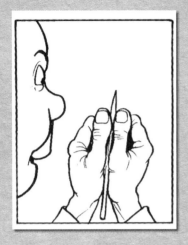

Here's how tae dae it. Pick a blade o' grass. It should hae a flat surface. Haud it between yer thumbs like this.

Whit fun we had. An auld man thocht we wis a pipe band. Grouser Gray jumped up a lamppost. He thocht we wis a racin' car!

An' a mother thocht she heard her baby greetin'!

So jist remember, if ye wannae be heard, blaw some squealers!

Part 9 - Stuff tae dae
Oor gang, jist like any ither, has some saicret codes.

Here's an important message in twa
different codes:
NFFU BU TIFE UPOGHIU
TEEM TA DEHS THGINOT

Fat Bob an' Soapy understood an' they came tae
the shed the nicht. How did they ken?

We're usin' a new code now, so I can tell ye
a saicret. In the first code, each letter has
been changed tae the letter next door in the
alphabet. In the second, each word has been
spelt back tae front. Simple, eh!

Ma next message wis
POA COT MTT UHI RIE DDS OE CY HE AR BC

This is mair difficult an' yer need tae ken ma saicret
code, if I can remember it. P.C. Murdoch couldna
manage to make sense o' it when he found it.

Here's how it works. Ma code word is "Wullies code".
Write it ower the top o' the page. Then write
each o' the groups o' letters in columns under it and
then read the message - braw, eh!

W	U	L	L	I	E	S	C	O	D	E
P	C	M	U	R	D	O	C	H	A	B
O	O	T	H	I	D	E	Y	E	R	C
A	T	T	I	E	S					

But now I've tellt ye that code as weel, I'll need tae
invent anither!
JVA IEB NNO GSA SHB CE RP IP VM

151

Codes

P.C. Murdoch has a new walkie-talkie. He didna get on wi' it, as it kept him tae busy!

Tae help him, I found the funny alphabet the polis use, an' gied him a Wullie version.

A	ALPHA	ARREST
B	BRAVO	BURGLAR
C	CHARLEE	CATTIE
D	DELTA	DETECTIVE
E	ECHO	ELEPHANT
F	FOXTROT	FISHIN'
G	GOLF	GROUSER GRAN
H	HOTEL	HAN'CUFFS
I	INDIA	INSPECTOR
J	JULIET	JEEMY
K	KILO	KICKING (FITBA')
L	LIMA	LAZY
M	MIKE	MURDOCH
N	NOVEMBER	NOTE BOOK
O	OSCAR	OOR WULLIE
P	PAPA	POLIS
Q	QUEBEC	QUIET
R	ROMEO	RASPBERRY
S	SIERRA	SWAG
T	TANGO	TROUBLE
U	UNIFORM	UMBRELLA
V	VICTOR	VIOLIN
W	WHISKY	NAE CHANGE NEEDED!
X	X-RAY	EXIT
Y	YANKEE	YE'LL BE GOIN' HAME, THEN
Z	ZULU	XYLOPHONE

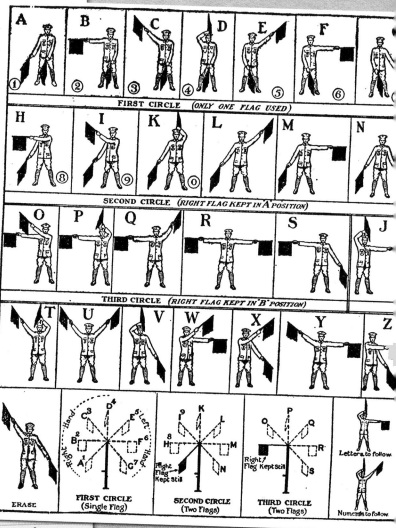

I hope this helps him — itherwise he'll hae tae use semaphore, an' that'll mak' him look silly.

Wullie's Fund-Raisin' Scheme

We dinnae hae new fangled radios but we hae tae dae something tae compete with P.C. Murdoch, so I made "Wullie's Walkie-Talkies".

Here's how tae mak' yer ain.

Ye'll need: some string an' twa tin cans or plastic drinkin' cups or yoghurt pots. Mak' sure there are nae jaggy edges on the tins.

Mak' twa holes in the bottom o' each can or pot. Thread the string through the holes an' secure wi' a knot on the base. If possible, thread the string through a button for best results.

Ane o' ye speaks intae the can and the ither puts the can tae his ear tae hear. Foolproof!

Nae sale, then. Next, I ran richt intae P.C. Murdoch an' broke his walkie-talkie.

153

Knots

Ye need tae use knots for a' sorts o' things.
These pics may help ye, even if they didna help me.

STRAPPED TO YOUR FRONT TO LOOK LIKE FAT BOAB.

MAKES A BRAW RABBIT TRAP.

Have you got any string?
"No, I'm a frayed knot."

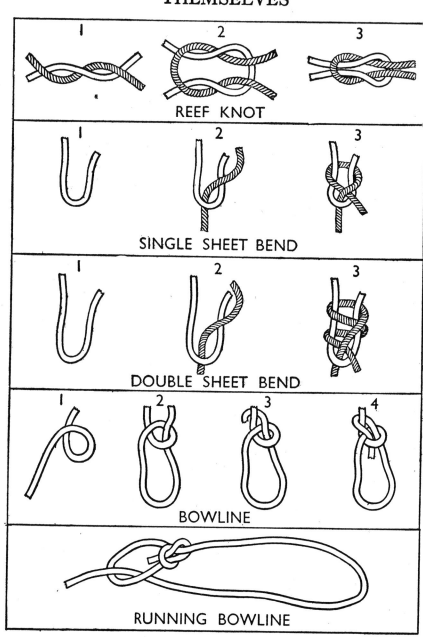

SOME SIMPLE KNOTS WHICH EXPLAIN THEMSELVES

REEF KNOT

SINGLE SHEET BEND

DOUBLE SHEET BEND

BOWLINE

RUNNING BOWLINE

Ye need tae ken knots tae make a lasso.

LATER
GIT ALONG LITTLE DOGIE!

~ YIPPEE! GOT HIM!

1   2

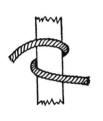

CLOVE HITCH

1   2   3

WHIPPING A ROPE'S END

1   2

CARRICK BEND

WULLIE'S WISDOMS

Tellin fibs will just get ye tied in knots!

Knot, knot!
Who's there?
Bowline.
Bowline who?
I'm goin' bowline ... want tae come wi' me?

MOORING HITCH

TWO HALF HITCHES

ROUND TURN AND TWO HALF HITCHES

HA-HA-HA!

STOP LAUGHIN'! HELP ME OOT O' THIS!

Makin' things wi' paper

There's mair ye can dae wi' paper than write on't — a paper plane is much mair interestin' than writin' homework. Here are some ideas.

Paper planes

The auld favourite — jist a wee reminder aboot how tae mak' it.

1. Tak' a sheet o' A4 paper, an' fold it in half langways.

2. Fold a corner doon tae the fold. Dae this for the ither side.

3. Fold this new fold doon tae the original fold — see ma picture. Dae this for both sides.

4. An' fold it again.

5. Hold the centre an' then fold the wings oot.

6. Now throw the plane!

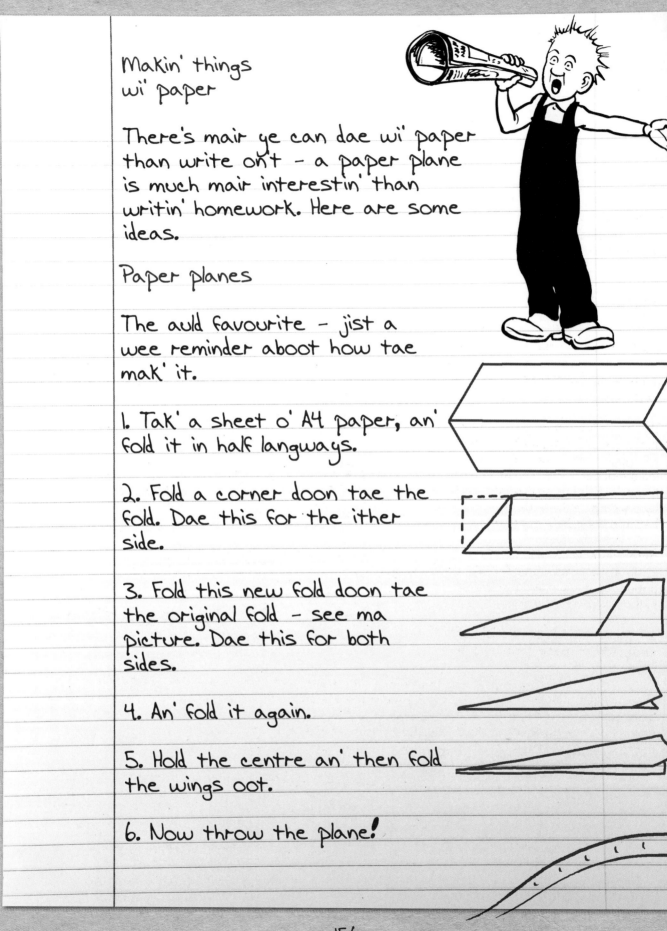

That wis easy! Here are some mair complicated planes

Making paper planes

One of the most important things about model aircraft is that they fly best when they are made in shapes that suit model sizes – not when they copy full-size aeroplane shapes.

Try making the paper plane shown here.

Start with an A4 sheet of paper. Follow the steps in the diagram. Some of the folds are a bit tricky, so take care.

The traditional paper dart will fly straighter and faster, but this model will glide better and will stay in the air longer. It can also be made to perform loops and aerobatics by bending up the ends of the tail because it is a better design.

Here are some more ideas to try
1. Make a smaller model of a paper dart and of this design using half an A4 sheet of paper.

2. Make a larger model of each, with a page torn from a newspaper.

The smaller model should fly quite well, but not as well as the first model you made. Try making them half as small again. This time the models will be poor flyers.

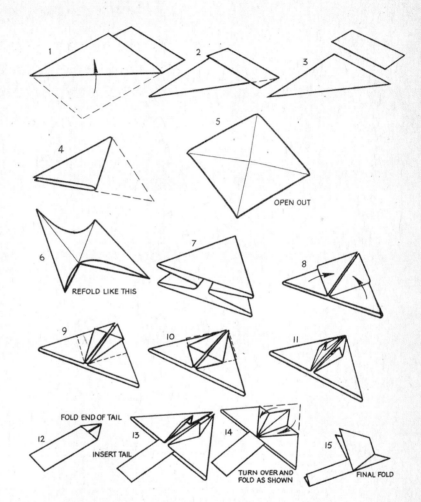

This seems to show that the larger the model the better. What happens, though, when you try to fly the newspaper size dart and aeroplane? They are so floppy that they hardly fly at all.

Using stiffer paper improves their performance, but paper is just not stiff enough for large flying models.

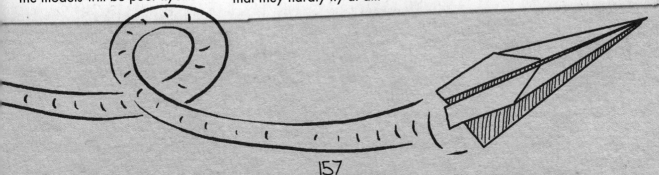

Sojer's hat

Here's jist whit a
sojer needs.

1. Tak' a sheet o' an auld
newspaper (mak' sure Ma an'
Pa dinnae need it).

2. Fold it in half.

3. Turn doon the corners
marked 'A' in ma plan below ala
the dotted line to the centre
('B').

If ye want tae
hae a sword,
try this.

Tear a strip
aboot 6 in.
(150 mm)
wide aff a
sheet o' a big
newspaper.
Roll it up fairly
loosely. Secure
the end wi' a
piece o' sticky
tape. Pull the
paper oot fae
the centre
o' the roll.
Now ye hae a
sword!

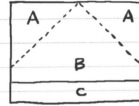

4. Fold up the bottom strip 'C';
aboot 2 in. (50 mm). Turn the
paper ower an' repeat the
bottom fold on the ither side.
See ma second drawin'.

5. Put both yer thumbs inside
the bottom openin' an' pull the
paper open, an' refold it so th
the dotted line in ma second
drawin' is on the ootside, the
edges A an' B formin' the centr
line on ither side. See ma third
drawin'.

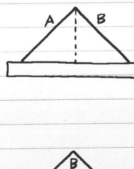

6. Fold alang the dotted line in
ma third drawin', bringin' A tae

7. Wear yer cap – an' obey
orders.

A fortune teller

Fat Bob had a fortune teller made o' paper, but it wisnae guid - it said I'd never mak' ony money! I've made ma ain and now I'm happy. Here's how tae mak' it.

1. Ye'll need a square piece o' paper at least 6 in. (150 mm) square.
2. Fold the square in half. Then fold it in half agin.
3. Press doon on the edges tae mak' a crease.
4. Open up the square an' then fold each corner intae the middle. Unfold an' leave the creases behind on the paper.
5. Turn the paper ower an' write the fortunes alang the edges - see ma drawin'.
6. Turn these four corners intae the centre an' crease the paper.
7. Write numbers ontae the flaps - an' o' course ye can count up tae 8.
8. Fold in half. Open up an' fold in half the ither way. Put yer twa thumbs an' big fingers under the flaps facing ye.

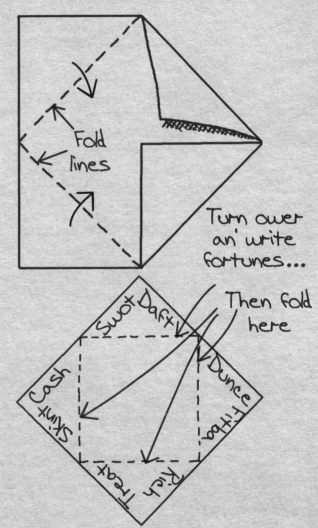

Fold lines

Turn ower an' write fortunes...

Then fold here

9. Ye can then move the pointy bits in twa ways, ane showin' numbers 1-4 an' ane showin' numbers 5-8.

I asked Fat Bob tae choose a number an' then move the fortune teller that number o' times. I dae it again an' then ask him tae pick a number. I turn ower the flap an' there is his fortune. Mak' a few fortune tellers so that ye can hae different fortunes for different people. Now whit would put in a fortune teller for P.C. Murdoch?

A tangram

Try makin' this tangram on a dreich day — ye can ither mak' it wi' thick paper or cardboard or wi' a bit o' plywood.

BOYS' WEEKLY

Make a tangram

Take a piece of cardboard or plywood that is 1 ft (300 mm) square. With a ruler mark out the square as shown in the diagram and cut it into pieces along the lines. Make each shape a different colour.

See if you can use the shapes to make a man and a dog.

The puzzle is thousands of years old and comes from China. It is called a tangram. There are hundreds of shapes to construct just using these pieces. here are a few examples. Some of these use an egg-shaped tangram. this is a bit harder to make, but can give more interesting shaps.

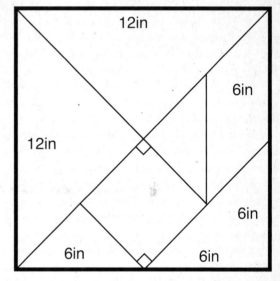

12in
12in
6in
6in
6in
6in

Wullie's Fund-Raisin' Scheme

I went tae the museum an' saw a' sorts o' modern art.

Some people pay money for picters like that. Time for me tae hae a go.

I drew a coo, a moose, a fish an' oor Provust McCrae and had an exhibishun.

BESSIE THE COO (COULDNA GO IN — THE BULL WIS THERE)

MOOSE (WIDNA COME OOT OF IT'S HOLE)

FISH (CAT BEAT ME TO IT)

PROVUST McCRAE (HE WIS HAVIN A SHAIV)

But ma art wisnae understood.

And ma public a' wanted their money back. Only P.C. Murdoch saw ma talent.

Whit's the time?

Ma keeps complainin' that I am late for ma meals, but how can I tell the time if I hae nae watch!

Me rushin' tae ma dinner

Ways o' tellin' the time

Sun dial (but nae sun at nicht – or maist days)
Toon clock
(but it disnae work)
Askin' P.C. Murdoch
(but he'd get fed up o' me askin')
Clock in kitchen
(but I need tae ken the time afore I get there)

Water clocks

↑ A bucket clock.

The Egyptians realised that sun clocks had one big disadvantage. When there was no sun the clock could not work. In order to measure time, day or night, rain or shine, it was necessary to build a clock that had nothing to do with the movement of the Earth or the Sun. The problem was solved by the invention of the water clock.

The Chinese used a bowl with a small hole in the bottom. They put the bowl in a tank of water. When the bowl filled with water, it sank. The man looking after the clock knew that an hour had passed. He rang a gong to tell everyone the time, emptied the bowl and started all over again. Later, the Chinese improved their clock. They placed a number of jars on steps. The top jar was filled with water, which ran down from one jar to the next.

The pictures show you how you could make these Chinese water clocks.

Collectin'

We a' collect the cards fae bubblegum, fae tea an' fae Pa an' his mates if they smoke cigarettes. Here are some o' my favoorites – I like footballers an' cars an' lorries an' adventure. I hae some for swappin' (cash preferred). An' I hope ye hae counted the number o' bucket cards in ma book. I still need some mair.

Museums hae collectshuns o' things an' I thocht I should help them. If I could gie them something, mebbe I could get ma name on a notice.

When I saw an auld vase bein' thrown away, I rescued it an' took it tae the museum.

He didna want it! As I left, I saw the cleaner's bucket is leakin'. Ken whit tae dae.

No.12

DOING ALL MY BEST THINKING ON.

LOTUS 7A

ASTON MARTIN DB 4

A.C. ACE

WONDERS OF ENGINEERING

Presented with
Bullseye Bubble Gum
No.1 Empire State Building

See back for details

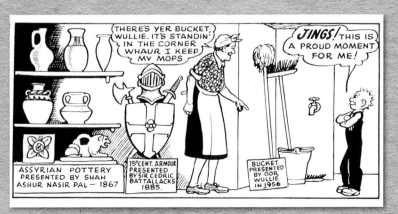

Magic tricks

I wis gien a conjurin' set for Christmas. It had lots o' tricks in it. It even showed me how tae cut a lady in twa. It wis real magic!

Wi' a bit mair practice, I'll become Wullie the Wizard, wi' ma magic wand.

Here are a few tricks tae impress yer friends wi'. Now get practisin' but dinna try tae trick me!

It's great how ye can swing a bucket fu' o' water roond yer heid an' yet no' spill a drap. See if ye can dae it, but no' inside yer hoose.

THE GREATEST MAGICIANS

Houdini was the greatest showman the world has ever known. He would be tied hand and foot, manacled, strapped in a straitjacket, suspended upside down from a crane, but from all these restraints he would walk away in the twinkling of an eye. How did he do it – well we don't really know. His secrets died with him.

Magic for beginners

No.32

Guess the date of a coin

Reach into your pocket, bring out a handful of coins.

Ask someone to pick out one, look at its date and remember it.

You then apparently concentrate very hard and say, 'The date you are thinking of is 1982,' and you are right.

How?

Simple. Make sure all the coins in your pocket have the same date. If you have arranged for a friend to have a number of coins that all have the same date and you ask the other person to look at one of the coins in your friend's pocket, then you have something that really appears to be mind reading.

Here's another tumbler trick! Ask your pals if they can stand a tumbler on a piece of paper which is laid across another tumbler.

Here's how it's done. Just fold the paper like this and —

HEY PRESTO!

MAGIC LINK

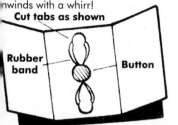

Here's how to make your chums jump! All you need is an elastic band, a button, some cardboard and an envelope. Put it all together as shown, then wind the elastic band up, carefully fold over the card, and pop it into the envelope. Then stand back and enjoy the fun when your pal opens the envelope and the button unwinds with a whirr!

Cut tabs as shown

Rubber band **Button**

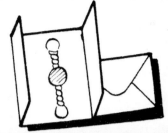

VANISHING EGG FROM EGG-CUP

A brightly-polished egg-cup containing an egg is introduced. Removing the egg, the hand makes a squeezing movement and gradually opens; the egg has entirely vanished! No skill required; no palming; no practice.

See reverse for full details.

TEAR A BIT

A novel paper tearing effect. A word is printed on a large strip of paper. After each tear there is a smile for a COMPLETE WORD always remains! After the last letter is torn the pieces are MAGICALLY RESTORED!! The comedy patter gives you a gag for every tear.

See reverse for full details.

TOPSY-TURVY GLASSES

Three glasses are set in a row on the table. The two outer glasses are upside down and the centre one is right way up. The problem is to turn over two tumblers at a time using both hands and in three moves only, so all three glasses are the right way up.

First of all, show that it can be done in three turns.
• Set the three glasses up in a row on the table, the centre one right way up and the two outer ones upside down.
• As they are facing you, take the two glasses on the left, one in each hand, and turn them over.
• Now cross your arms and turn over the two outside glasses.
• Now once again turn over the two glasses on the left.
• Having done it once, offer to do it again, in slow motion, just in case anyone has not quite got the hang of it.

Invite a spectator to have a go. But no matter how often he or she tries to duplicate your moves, they cannot get all three glasses the right way up in three moves.

Why is it impossible for a spectator to duplicate this? The first and most important reason is this: having done the effect once or twice, you finish up with all three glasses right way up on the table. Having done this, you turn the centre glass upside down and ask a spectator to try his or her luck. Have you noticed the difference? When you did it, you started with the centre glass right way up and the other two inverted, but when you ask the spectator to try it the three glasses are the other way round. The centre glass is inverted and the outer glasses are the right way up. It is a strange but true fact that most people will not spot the difference.

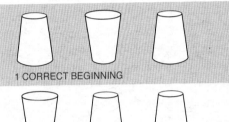

1 CORRECT BEGINNING

2 FIRST MOVE - TWO LEFT HAND GLASSES TURNED OVER

3 SECOND MOVE - TWO END GLASSES OVER WITH CROSSED HANDS. RIGHT HAND TAKES LEFT-HAND GLASS AND VICE-VERSA

4 THIRD MOVE - TWO LEFT-HAND GLASSES ARE TURNED OVER

5 TURN OVER CENTRE GLASS AND INVITE SOMEONE TO TRY

Magic for beginners

Think of a number

Ask someone to:
• Think of a number.
• Double it.
• Add eight.
• Halve it.
• Subtract the number he or she first thought of from this total.

Tell them that the number he or she first thought of is four.

The number being thought of will always be half the number you ask them to add – so always make sure you ask them to add an even number!

But whit if ma wee Jockie didnae re-appear again?

THE MAGIC MATCHBOX

To prepare. All that is required is a matchbox, which is prepared in the following way. A small slit is cut with a sharp knife along one edge of the tray of the matchbox. The diagram shows this. That is all the preparation needed for the magic matchbox.

The effect is simple.
• You show a matchbox.
• Open the drawer and place a five pence coin into the box.
• You close the drawer of the box.
• Give the box a shake, and your spectator will hear the coin rattling inside the box.
• Hand over the box and ask your spectator to open the box and when he or she does so, they will be surprised to find that the five pence has changed to a ten pence coin.

How is it done? The illustration gives the game away. When the five pence coin is placed into the

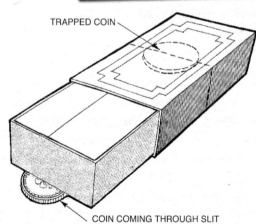

TRAPPED COIN

COIN COMING THROUGH SLIT

box it is pushed through the slit and straight out into your left hand. The box is closed immediately and shaken to allow the spectator to hear it rattling. Actually, the coin that your spectator can hear rattling is the ten pence coin that, as you will see from the illustration, is trapped between the top of one end of the drawer and the outer cover of the box. As soon as the drawer is closed the coin drops into the drawer.

INDIAN YOGI

The famous Fire Eating effect used by oriental performers. This is the true professional method. A quantity of cotton fibre is placed in the mouth which produces sparks and clouds of smoke from the performer's mouth. Fire proof protection. Large supply of ingredients required and clear, easy instructions. QUITE HARMLESS AND EASY TO DO.

SAFETY PIN THROUGH HANKY

A spectator pins a safety pin through a borrowed hanky. The performer holds the pin and it passes in a flash through the hanky. Pin is NOT undone. Person holding the hanky is most mystified of all. Pin is removed still tightly fastened.

See reverse for full details.

SIMPLICITY ROPE TRICK

Take a length of rope and tie the ends together. A spectator is asked to cut the loop fairly and squarely in the centre. When this is done the magician trims the ends off the knot and squeezes it. To the astonishment of the audience –

THE ROPE IS COMPLETELY WHOLE AGAIN!

See reverse for full details.

Magic for beginners

No. 12

Magic numbers

Write down on a sheet of paper the number 12,345,679.
- Ask someone to give you any single digit.
- Suppose they say 5.
- You immediately ask them to multiply the number 12,345,679 by 45.
- While they are doing the sum tell them that the answer is 555,555,555.

How so?

When they give you a number multiply it by 9. Tell them to multiply the large number by this figure. The answer will always be made up only of the number they first gave you.

I wonder if Primrose would volunteer for the real thing?

April Fool

Naebody will mak' a fool o' me on April Fool's Day!

"Wullie! You've forgotten your schoolbooks."

"Look Wullie! There's some money on the pavement!"

"Wullie – your bootlace is loose!"

"Hey, Wullie, You're being followed!"

WULLIE'S LIST O' TRICKS
"Yer bicycle's got a puncture!"
"Look, Ma, there's a coo in the gairden!"
"They're giein' awa' free sweets at the shop!"
"There's a dug behind ye!"
"We won the fitba' cup!" (we never dae.)
"Yer back's a' dirty!"

A' tricks, o' course, until I got tae school an' the teacher gied me lines for no' haein' ma school books, for haein' an untied bootlace, an' for bein' followed by a dug. I had tae write ma lines in ink an' ma pen ran oot.

Magnets

Ye can hae lots o' fun wi' a magnet. Ye can attract metal things, ye can sort metals fae no'-magnetic things – ye' find some metals, like aluminium, are no' magnetic.

I found a horseshoe magnet. Naebody wis pleased wi' me and ma magnet.

P.C. Murdoch had taken his tacketty boots aff tae rest his feet . . .

Then Mr McCay offered me a cuppy in an auld tin can . . .

Next it wis Gernie Green wi' her hair in a bun . . .

Crivvens, the magnet had the last laugh. It got ma bucket . . .

Wullie's Fund-Raisin' Scheme

Jings, it wis a cauld winter an' I really wanted a pair o' skates. But guess whit — I hadna ony money.

I had a braw idea — tae dae portable hot water bottles for fowk who had tae be outside in the cauld.

I found auld hot water bottles and onything rubber, like fitba' bladders, that could haud water.

There were lots o' happy fowk that day, an' I made enuff tae buy the skates.

Tae keep me warm I filled a bicycle tyre inner-tube.

Trouble wis, a'body wanted tae warm their hands an' their weight caused the ice tae crack . . .

I'll dae nae mair hot-water bottle sellin'!

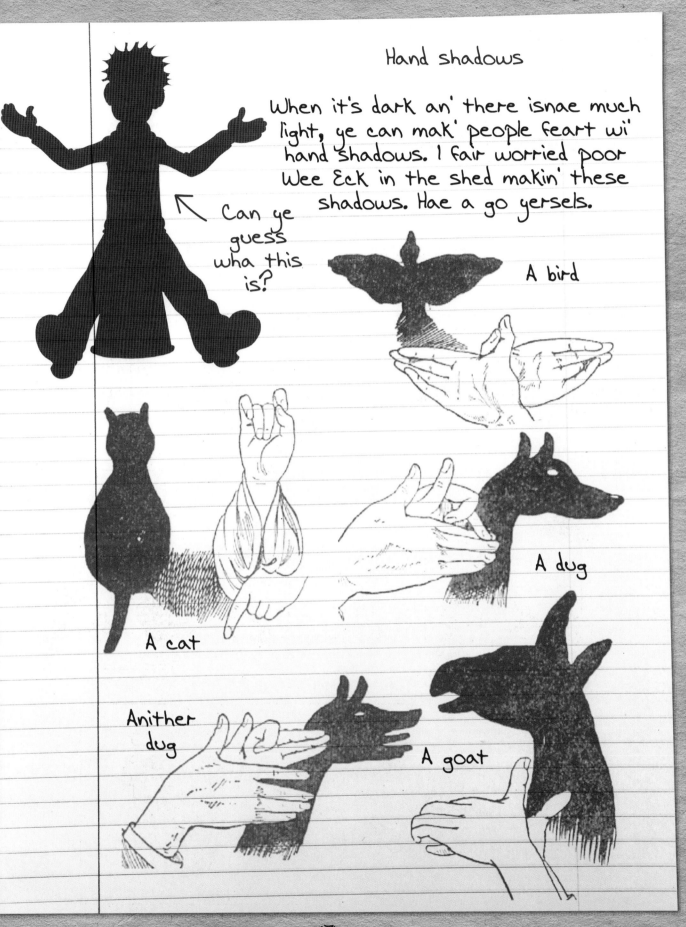

Hand shadows

When it's dark an' there isnae much light, ye can mak' people feart wi' hand shadows. I fair worried poor Wee Eck in the shed makin' these shadows. Hae a go yersels.

Can ye guess wha this is?

A bird

A cat

A dug

Anither dug

A goat

The New Year

Hand shadows helped in ma New Year celebrashuns. I put up a notice tellin' a'body tae go tae ma shed an' no' the hoose. Ma an' Pa were puzzled that naebody came tae see them. We had a' the fun in the shed. It wis braw!

Next day Ma an' Pa asked tae see ma New Year Resolushuns. The list had tae include

NAE MAIR PARTIES IN THE SHED.

Afore I wrote them, I had a busy mornin'. Can ye guess whit I wis doin'? It made writing the Resolushuns easier.

MA NEW YEAR RESOLUSHUNS
NAE KICKING BASHER WHEN HE'S NO' LOOKIN'.
NAE PULLIN' JESSIE DICK'S PIGTAILS.
NAE NOCKIN' AFF P.C. MURDOCH'S HELMET (AYE RICHT).
NAE RINGIN' GRUMPY GREEN'S DOOR BELL AN' RUNNIN' AWAY.
NAE WRITIN' POEMS ABOOT TEACHER.
NAE SCARIN' LASSES WI' MA CLOCKWORK MOOSE.
NAE WAERIN' OOT O' MA BOOTS ON ICY SLIDES.

Ma an' Pa were suspishous, so I had tae write some mair. I thocht I would resolve tae dae things in the hoose that didna need doin' anyway. Clever, eh

MA NEW YEAR RESOLUSHUNS AGAIN

HELP MA WI' THE DISHE (she'll never trust me

PRESS PA'S PANTS (they dinnae need pressing)

LIGHT THE FIRE EVERY MORNIN' (Ma uses a electric fire)

FILL MA'S HOT WATER BOTTLE (Ma has a electric blanket now)

But they tricked me intae doin' things. Ma had me dae lots o' washin' up wi' unbreakable plates an' Pa had me pressin' the pants o' the whole fitba' team. The cheek o' it!!

Here's ma final word on resolushuns.

MA NEW YEAR RESOLUSHUNS YET AGAIN

I RESOLVE TAE MAKE NAE MORE RESOLUSHUNS.

173

The Carnival

The start o' the New Year is the time for the Carnival, a magic indoor fair, with lots o' braw rides an' a' sorts of side shows. I bashed Pa aroond on the dodgems, flew doon the helter skelter an' got turned roond an' roond on the whirler. I didna feel like eatin' a hot dug after that ride!

There were lots o' stalls that offered prizes. Ma fishin' skills helped wi' "Hook a Duck" and ma cattie skills should ha' made "Knock Off Cans" richt easy – but I missed (must dae some mair practice afore next year).

Stalls tae try an' win at

    Skittles
    Hoop-la
    Beat the Goalie
    Ball in the Bucket
    Knock Off Cans

Rides tae dream aboot
    The Ghost Train
    The Dropzone
    The Roller Coaster
    The Auld Waltzer –
      jist for Ma
    The Octopus Spinner

FREE WITH THE BEEZER

The WHIRLY WHIZZER RRRRRRRRR

Aye, ma heid jist spins aroond thinkin' o' a' the fun in store next year!

I must dae some cattie practice the morrow.

But Pa tellt me nae tae. Whit a day. I wis tempted by...

...bottles

...men wearin' top hats

...a bull's eye in a shop windie.

But I couldna resist firin' at a chimney.

Jings, whit'll Pa say! I ran aff at top speed.

I now ken that he wud hae laughed a lot. I fooled masel!

Well, that wis enocomical wi' the truth. Here's whit really happened. →

After P.C. Murdoch confiscated ma cattie, I tempted him wi' some braw cattie targets. He didna ken it wis me makin' the targets.

At last he could resist nae mair, an' I wis ready.

I've ma cattie back, now, an' can practise for the Carnival.

Wullie's Fund-Raisin' Scheme

I need tae find ma ladder. Then I can pay for more rides at the Carnival. I dinna think Pa thocht aboot that when he gied me the ladder tae clean the windies, but I saw a business opportunity!

Things ye can dae wi' a ladder

Help fowk climb a wall tae watch the fitba'.

Convert it intae a see-saw tae keep kids happy.

Deliver parcels

Make it intae a hammock

Aye, an' get tae the top o' the ladder!

The Wild West

I am the deid-eye shot in the wild west o' Auchenshoogle wi' ma cattie, but it a'ways gets me thinkin' o' the real Wild West.

10   Western Chronicle, June 23, 1955

> **"A man's got to have a code, a creed to live by, no matter his job."**
>
> John Wayne

THE COWBOY CODE

★ Don't pass anyone on the trail without giving them a nod and saying "Howdy Pardner".

★ If you are coming up on someone from behind, give a yell of greeting before you get within gunshot range.

★ Don't wave at a cowboy on his horse. It might scare the horse. Just nod.

★ If you pass someone on the trail, don't turn and look back. He might think you don't trust him.

★ Never shoot an unarmed man.

★ Defend yourself if necessary.

★ Don't make threats unless you are ready for the consequences.

★ Always give a warning before you pull the trigger. This is "the rattlesnake code" to be followed unless you are stalking, when it can be ignored.

★ A cowboy is pleasant at all times.

★ A cowboy always helps someone in need, whether stranger, friend or foe.

★ Never take another man's horse. A horse thief will be hung.

★ Never try on another man's hat.

★ Never try to wake up another cowboy by touching him, or shaking him. He will possibly wake up with a start, pull out his gun and shoot you.

★ A cowboy never talks too much; save your breath for breathing.

★ After a long hard day in the saddle, look after your horse before you feed yourself.

★ Remove your guns before taking your place at the dining table.

★ Complain about the cooking and you might become the cook.

★ Don't wake up the wrong cowboy for his shift, you might get shot. Cowboys need their rest.

★ Always drink with your glass in your gun hand to show your intentions are friendly.

★ Honesty is the code - your word is your bond, a handshake involving spitting on to your hand before shaking, is more binding than any fancy lawyer's contract.

But if you look back an' he looks back an' he sees you lookin' back an' you see him lookin' back - whit dae ye dae then? Just shoot each ither?

WULLIE'S WISDOMS

Don't squat on yer heels when you're wearin' spurs

AUCHENSHOOGLE POLICE STATION
DATE ..... *Sunday 16th*
POLICE CONSTABLE ..... *Murdoch*

*Sunday – On patrol, all quiet.
Then an emergency call from the
Town Hall – it was a bad line –
something about somebody with
guns trying to steal their horse? I
called for backup and the firearms
team, but before they arrived,
I brought the situation under
control. It was Wild Wullie and his
dangerous gang of horse stealers.
I disarmed them and confiscated
their spurs.*

*"Get off that
statue at
once"*

179

PART 12 - Ma favoorite food

Ma says that a growin' lad a'ways needs food, but I ken she dishae ken the meanin' o' "a'ways". How can a jeely piece when I git back fae school "spoil ma tea" when she kens that it's jist getting' ma tummy in trainin'.

A word aboot bread
It's no easy tae cut bread evenly - Ma's a'ways on aboot the strange shape I leave a loaf in.

Wullie's guide tae jeely pieces

1. Find the bread, the bread board an' the bread knife.

2. Cut a slice o' bread. Make sure it's good an' thick, but not so thick it willnae fit intae yer mooth.

3. Spread it wi' butter.

4. Then cover it wi' strawberry jam, or honey, or treacle or whitever ye fancy. Ye can even pretend tae be American an' spread it wi' peanut butter an' strawberry jam thegither (I'm no' jokin').

Whit could be simpler than that?

If ye jist hae sliced bread, ye need at least six slices tae make a decent piece.

If ye only hae that French bread which is lang an' thin, cut it sidey-ways tae get the biggest piece ye can!

Once made, take it tae yer shed or room an' enjoy yer piece in peace.

Food is probably the maist important thing when I'm awake.

If I had a guest hoose or a wee hotel, this wuid be the menu –

Wullie's Dinin' Rooms

Open a' day, every day, except when closed

BREAKFAST 2/6d
Porridge
Ham and Eggs / Bacon and Runny Eggs
Bread, Toast & Marmalade

DINNER 3/6d
Soup o' the day : Pea Soup or Scotch Broth
Mince Tatties & Peas
Puddin' o' the day : Semolina Puddin' or Bread &
Butter Puddin' or Ice Cream

TEA 3/6d
Fish an' Chips
A piece wi' Strawberry Jam
Cream Cookie or Raising Buns or Cherry Cake

TAE DRINK
Skoosh 6d, Sasparrillo 6d, Ginger 6d
Pot o' tea 1/–

PLEASE TIP GENEROUSLY WHEN ORDERIN' SO THE
MAINAGEMENT KEN TAE GIE YE PROPRIAT SERVICE

CASH ONLY, NAE FOREIGN COINS, NAE CREDIT, AND
DINNAE STEAL THE KNIVES & FORKS.
NAE DOGGIE BAGS.

Ma wanted her recipes for twa o' ma favoorites, Mince, Tatties an' Peas an' Scotch Broth tae go intae the book, so ye a' can enjoy them, too. That's braw, Ma!

One o' ma Wullie's favourites is Mince, Tatties and Peas. He's eaten it so often, it has helped tae make him the boy he is. Try it for yourselves (or get someone tae cook it for you).

MINCE, TATTIES & PEAS

To make the Mince:
1 lb of mince
2 chopped onions
1 oz of butter (that's a dod)
2 chopped carrots
1 oz of plain flour
Beef stock or gravy

Cook the onions in the butter, in the pot, until they are soft.

Add the mince, mash it up and separate the bits and then brown it until you can't see any pink bits. You'll need a wooden spoon to do this.

Chop up the carrots and add them to the mince – can be circles or wee bits – circles are better.

Sprinkle the flour in and mix it well in.

You'll need beef stock or gravy (enough liquid to cover the mince) – you can mix up a gravy powder from a packet or use a stock cube by doing what it says on the instructions.

If you don't have stock or gravy, you can use water, but be sure to add a wee bit of salt and pepper.

Cook the mince gently till it is tender and the carrots are soft and the gravy is nice and thick – for about an hour. Serve with heaps of mashed tatties and enough peas till they start falling off the plate.

To make the Tatties:

2lb of floury potatoes, peeled and cut into chunks (Should be enough for 4, depends how hungry you are)
¼ pint (150 ml) milk
A dod of butter
Salt & pepper

Floury potatoes like Maris Pipers or King Edwards make the best mash.

Peel 2lb of tatties and cut them up into chunks and cook them in a large pan of boiling salted water, cover with a lid and simmer for 20-25 minutes. (Simmering is gentle bubbles).

Drain the tatties, by holding the lid just off the edge, enough to let the water out, without scalding yourself, and keep the tatties in the pan.

Warm up about ¼ pint of milk and pour over the tatties and mash until smooth, with a wee dod of butter. Serve immediately.

To make the Peas:

Peas straight from the pod are best. Take the peas out of the pods just before you are ready to cook them, but it can take a wee while if ye keep eating them raw.

All you need to do is boil them for 2 to 3 minutes, or until they are just tender.

Fresh peas or frozen ones from a bag are great. If you're stuck, try some frenchies (petit pois from a tin!) Rare! Just heat them up – they come in their ain juice.

SCOTCH BROTH

How to make Scotch Broth

You need to ask the butcher for a neck of lamb.
3 pints (1.7 litres) of water
1 oz (25 g) of pearl barley
2 oz (50 g) of dried peas
2 diced carrots (that means chopped into wee bits)
1 finely chopped onion
1 big sliced leek
1 small turnip, diced up
4 oz (100g) of kail (cabbage), shredded finely
1 tablespoon of parsley, chopped up

Soak the peas and barley overnight.

The next day, in a pan filled with 3 pints of water, put in the lamb, peas, barley and some seasoning (seasoning is salt and pepper) and boil it for one hour.

Skim the surface to get the scummy stuff off, and then add the carrots, turnip, onion and leek and boil for another 15 minutes.

Take out the lamb and break it up into wee bits before putting it back in the pot.

Skim off any fat and then serve with chopped parsley.

This makes around enough for 6 plates of soup.

Ma is the bestest cook in the world. Even better at Scotch Broth than Maw Broon!

Scotch Broth is my favoorite soup - it's like a meal in itsel' and Ma says "it goes a long way". (Never gets further than the table in oor hoose!)

Guid pairty manners

Sometimes the problem is whit tae demolish first. Ice cream first otherwise it'll mak' an awfy mess an' ye'll waste it doon yer dungarees. Never be greedy. Ye need tae hae guid manners. Only ever take as much as you can possibly eat. Best tae grab as much as ye can, as soon as ye can at pairties, in case Fat Bob's there.

101 THINGS TAE DAE WI' A BUCKET

No. 34

SOOK!

HOLDING A WULLIE-SIZED PORTION OF SARSAPARILL

The secret tae the best biled egg :

Put it in the cold water, a when it starts tae bile (gen mind or ye'll crack it), put y toast in an' turn the dial tae minutes. When the toast po Bob's yer uncle an' yer egg just richt for sojers

There's nuthin' better than a wee snack at bedtime – a hot water bottle, the papers an' a mug o' hot chocolate. Braw !

WULLIE'S WISDOMS

If ye want breakfast in bed, sleep in the kitchen.

184

I like ma biled eggs tae be runny, but at Easter yer need tae hae hard-biled eggs for egg rollin'.
This year the yolk wis on me!

Sweets

Many's the time I've walked past the sweetie factory in oor toon an' wondered whit happens inside. One day ma dream came true!

It wis magic. There wis heaps o' sherbet,

an' trucks o' caramels,

MA FAVOORITE
SWEETS

SUGARELLY BUTTONS
SHERBET SOOKERS
MA'S TABLET
TOFFEE
CARAMELS
CHOCLATE BARS
BOILIN'S
EDINBURGH ROCK
TREACLE DABS

WULLIE'S WISDOMS

The ball is in your court. Can I hae it back?

an' great heaps o' boilin's,

an' a mountain o' Edinburgh Rock an' skyscrapers o' chocolate bars!

It wis amazin' — an' we didnae touch a sweet as we went roond. The nice man gied us each a bag o' the sweets they were makin' that day.

Pity we didnae like them. Still Granpaw Broon an' his pals did, an' they gied us money tae buy oor ain favoorites!

wonder if he's related tae Lord Snooty?

PART 11 – Survivin' school

I'm nearly at the end o' ma book, an' school's aboot tae start again.

GLUM

THINGS I DINNA LIKE ABOOT SCHOOL

TEACHERS
EXAMS, SWOTS
ARITHMETIC
SPELLIN' TESTS
REPORTS
LEARNIN' POEMS
WRITIN' LINES

THINGS I LIKE ABOOT SCHOOL MA FRIENDS

PLAYIN' BOOLS

MEETIN' AULD ENEMIES
STARIN' OOT THE WINDIE
PLAYIN' FITBA'
DAEING WELL

HOMEWORK
THE JANNY

TRICKIN' THE JANNY
PLAYIN' CONKERS

PLAYIN' TRICKS

Homework

Naebody likes daeing homework Sometimes ye canna dae it in time. Ye may need an excuse for the teacher. Try ony o' these.

MA FAVOORITE EXCUSES

YE ASKED FAE IT TAE BE DONE BY WEDNESDAY – I DIDNA KEN YE MEANT THIS WEDNESDAY

$159 + 28 - 21$ AND 42 GOES INTO 189 AND DIVIDE $72\frac{18}{24}$ BY $3\frac{6}{11}$.

PA COULDNA DAE IT

ARRY, MA DUG, RAN UA' WI' IT AN' BURIED IN THE GAIRDEN

I PUT MA JEELY PIECE DOON ON IT AN' IT'S A' STICKY AN' SPOLIED

P.C. MURDOCH CONFISCATED MA SCHOOL BAG

I LEFT IT IN THE LIBRARY

REFERENCE AND LENDING LIBRARY

IT GOT STUCK TAE THE TABLE WHERE I MAKE MA MODELS

I COULDNA READ MA AIN WRITIN'

HE'S BUSY DOING HIS HOMEWORK HIMSELF!

I RAN OOT O' SPACE IN MA BOOK

Exams

I dinna like exams. The best way tae miss an exam is tae be ill (or tae pretend tae be ill). Try some o' these ideas.

FALL IN THE BURN
GET SOME SNEEZIN'
POWDER
USE SOME FLOUR TAE
MAKE YER FACE WHITE
TELL MA YER THROAT HURTS
TELL MA YER HEID ACHES
TELL MA YER TUMMY'S SORE
GO TAE BED EARLY
(THEN MA AND PA WILL
THINK YOU ARE ILL)
PRETEND YE HAE A
SPAINED WRIST EFTER A
CARTIE ACCIDENT AN' CANNA
WRITE
STAND IN A CAULD DRAUGHT

Wullie
Had tae gather the troops the day. P.C. Murdoch needs a hand tae pass an exam and mebbe if he disnae pass — he'll get his jotters! So we tellt him a' the tips an' tricks that we ken aboot exams. He wasnae best pleased aboot cheatin' — but what I learned in ma history test is that it's best just tae write doon the answers ower an' ower again!

AUCHENSHOOGLE POLICE STATION
DATE Monday 28th
POLICE CONSTABLE Murdoch

That new Inspector's a pain. I've to go to a refresher course at the Police College about Community Policing (as if I don't know anything about that!) and there's an exam at the end of it! I just think I'm a bit long in the tooth to be learning new fangled things. They've sent loads of papers to read, new names for things – abbreviations to learn – call signs – and I'm not making any headway learning it.

Ma way a' learnin' dates

Cheatin's nae so guid. I found a piece o' paper wi' the answers tae a history test under teacher's desk. Whit should I dae?

I gied in an' memorised the answers. I didna hear teacher say it would be the geography test no' the history test the day.

I'll nae cheat again. It wis a sore experience.

An' then, afore ye ken, it's the holidays again.